THE PEOPLE DEMAND

THE PEOPLE DEMAND

PETER LANE

Typeset in Fanwood by Opitus Books

Cover by Park Designs

ISBN 9781838003586

Also available as an ebook, ISBN 9781838003593

First published by Opitus Books, United Kingdom, 2022.
www.opitus.uk.com

CONTENTS

ONE

Nasir Khalid Faisal Raziq was walking down May 23rd Street. He was 29 years old and dressed in the western style; straight cut jeans, casual shirt and trainers. His moustache and beard were trimmed short or perhaps he just hadn't shaved for a week. From a distance he looked stylish but closer up you could see that the clothes were past their best and his shoes were almost worn out.

Nasir was a part-time university lecturer, teaching an English Studies course for a few hours a week, except that the university had been closed for over a year after the authorities announced the discovery of a plot by Al-Qaeda affiliates to blow it up, along with as many students and staff as possible. No one was ever arrested or charged over the plot and there had been no terrorist activity in that part of the country since but the university remained shut, its students dispersed.

May 23rd Street was rather seedy. Its elegant buildings dating from the colonial era had been allowed to become dilapidated to such an extent that some of them were falling down, while those that weren't needed, at the very least a good lick of paint. Most of the once fashionable shops, some of them with international names, had closed down. Some remained empty, while others had been taken over by local traders and now sold cheap Bangladeshi-made shirts and underwear or other shoddy goods. The former king had encouraged this process of dilapidation by encouraging his subjects to avoid the vestiges of colonial rule like May 23rd and to shop in the traditional souks instead. This was in an attempt, unsuccessful as it happened, to gain credibility and popularity by dissociating himself from the foreigners who had installed him in power in the first place.

Not much was happening on May 23rd Street as Nasir walked down it. A couple of illegal money changers were at work, approaching the few tourists that ventured along it with fat wads of notes and offers of local currency at nearly twice the official rate. This was in full view of the local uniformed police who turned a blind eye, presumably in order to be given their cut later. The police were woefully poor at their jobs but looked quite impressive in their smart uniforms and with all that lethal weaponry on display. One of the policemen was a neighbour of Nasir's and he crossed the road to greet him with a smile and say a few words. Nasir knew that he almost certainly reported on anything and everything he and his neighbours did and everybody in the neighbourhood disliked him for it but he also knew that some of these same neighbours were paid informers of the Regime; every district, every street, had its informers.

With the university closed and no salary coming in, Nasir had had to find other ways to support himself and his family. In this he was luckier than most, since he spoke fluent English, as well as Arabic and French. He had built up a small clientele of people wanting tuition in English and there was also work to be had in translating documents, and in interpreting for foreign businessmen and diplomats and at conventions. At all this he was skilled but the work was erratic. He missed the campus environment and the regular university pay cheques. Having so much contact with foreigners, especially in the diplomatic missions, had its advantages but also its drawbacks; Nasir knew that it marked him out and made him the focus of regime attention. His room had been searched on more than one occasion and papers and the computer seized.

Nasir was on his way to the bus depot in order to ride to the Special Zone which was about fifteen miles away and on the Mediterranean coast. The Special Zone was actually a restricted zone open only to foreigners and those with special permits. It served two functions. Partly it was an economic zone which had been developed to promote industrial production by allowing foreign companies to import raw materials and parts and then to export finished goods, all free of local taxes and duties. Not all the companies there were foreign however, some were owned by relatives of members of the Regime, including three by brothers of the wife of the President.

Partly also, the Zone was a holiday destination with about a dozen luxury resorts and package hotels and accompanying bars, cafés and shops, all strung out along the best ten miles of coastline the country had and now out of bounds to most of its citizens. Within this resort area the usual strict rules regarding beach wear, alcohol and gambling did not apply, although the line was drawn at topless sunbathing. While the resort was supposedly built to encourage European tourists (it had its own airport connecting to several European cities), many of the beach goers were nationals, especially at weekends. The country's elite had no problems in obtaining permits, indeed the award of one was often the reward for some special favour towards the Regime. Nasir, however, had his permit because some of his language clients lived or worked in the Zone. The fact that it came through almost immediately he had applied for it indicated that the father of the child to whom he was to give English lessons, was high up and had pulled a few strings.

To reach the bus depot Nasir had to turn left off 23rd May. As he did so, he glanced backwards momentarily and noticed a car moving much too slowly. The initial feeling of panic gradually subsided. Nobody was going to grab him there, in broad daylight. There were too many people about, too many people with mobile phones with cameras to record the event and upload it onto Facebook or Twitter. Mobile phones and the internet had forced the DSI to change its ways. In the old days it had wanted people to know about its methods to serve as a warning. So raids were done in the daytime at the victim's home or they were picked up in the street and bundled into one of the regulation Citroens that everybody recognised. Then there would be an agonised wait, sometimes days, sometimes weeks, for the victim to be returned, body and spirit broken by torture, or as a corpse, dumped on the road. Too much of that had turned up online to allow it to continue, too many reports from Human Rights Watch, too many letters from Amnesty. So the DSI changed its ways, changed its favoured car and conducted its business with a little more subtlety, a little less bravado. Actually it wasn't called the DSI anymore. The Département de la Sécurité Intérieur had become the State Intelligence Agency years before but everyone still called it the DSI. Its address had been officially re-designated too but everyone still knew it as Number 42.

Nasir walked on for a good minute until he came to a café. He went in, ordered a short coffee and a sweet pastry and sat down at a table next to a window that enabled him to see back down the street outside. Presently the same car came into view and stopped a few yards before the café. It wasn't a Citroen but that didn't prove anything, and its windows were darkened so he couldn't tell how many people were inside. Nasir's fears returned. Once, as a naive student, he had spent two days in No 42. He still had the occasional nightmare. His mistake was to have taken part in a small demonstration in support of a lecturer who had been dismissed for making a derogatory remark about the President in one of his lectures. For most of those two days he had been kept alone in a darkened cell, with just the occasional interrogation and beatings with a leather strap. The lashes to his back and to the soles of his feet were excruciatingly painful but caused no lasting injury. What was worse was the cries of other detainees, obviously subject to more serious abuse, which could be heard at various times of the day and night. Nasir had wondered if such treatment lay ahead for him too but his ordeal came to a sudden end at the end of the second day when a guard opened his cell and announced his release. In the end Nasir concluded that it had just been a warning of what might lay in store should he repeat his error. Ironically, the incident just made this more likely since Nasir's anger at his treatment awakened an interest in politics where none had existed before. His torturers had demanded to know the names of other dissidents. Nasir could not give any names because he didn't know any dissidents then. He did now.

Nasir drank his coffee slowly and considered his options. A text to an associate, using the code to indicate that he was in danger, was a necessity. It would cause alarm but would also trigger the necessary response should he not return home at the usual time. Nasir took out his phone and sent the message. Then he called out to the owner to ask if there was a toilet. He was directed to a door at the side. The toilet was dirty and smelt foul but the flush worked, which was what Nasir wanted. He took out a small memory stick, broke it in two and then dropped it in. Then he covered it with a few of the torn up sheets of magazine that served as toilet paper and flushed it all away. Back at his table Nasir wondered whether to ask if there was a back door he could use but that might only get the owner into trouble and would not prevent his detention. If they were after him they would get him wherever he was. He had no means of permanent escape. The only real option was to leave the café and take whatever was coming. At least he'd got rid of the memory stick. That would have really landed him in it. Nasir walked to the counter and paid his bill. As he did so the car began to move slowly forward until it was adjacent to the café. Then it stopped.

As the café door closed behind him Nasir stood still, waiting and trembling slightly. The rear passenger window of the car unwound.

"Hello, Mr Raziq. May we offer you a lift? We are on our way to the Special Zone."

The smiling face was that of the Vice President of the Republic. Nasir recognised him immediately and could hardly believe his eyes. His surprise must have been evident.

"Yes, it is me, my driver too, Raffi. Everyone knows Raffi. Wind your window down and show yourself, Raffi."

The nearside front window unwound and the driver turned towards Nasir and smiled. It wasn't a pretty smile, more sinister really, for Raffi's left cheek had basically been shot away many years before, and the damage, despite plastic surgery, had left him permanently disfigured. It happened when would-be assassins or kidnappers had held up the Vice Presidential car on a lonely stretch of road outside of the capital. In the gun battle that ensued Raffi had wounded and successfully fought off the two assailants before driving his passenger to safety, even though he himself had been shot in the face and shoulder. Raffi spent weeks in hospital hovering between life and death before he began to recover. During that time the incident was given maximum publicity and he was hailed, and later decorated by the President, as a Hero of the Republic. It was true that everybody did know or could, at least, recognise Raffi.

"Please don't be alarmed, Mr Raziq. I would like to have a talk with you and I have a commercial proposition to make. Please be assured, you are in no danger. Won't you get in?"

Nasir hesitated before answering.

"Is it Number 42? Is that where I'm going? Do I have a choice?"

"Good heavens man! Do you think that the Vice President personally carts people off to prison? Of course you have a choice. You can get in or not as you wish. I want to talk to you about English lessons for a relative."

The Vice President opened the car door as he spoke.

"See, Mr Raziq, no one else, no weapons, no danger. Now will you please get in and allow me to save you a little time and money by driving you to the Special Zone?"

Nasir got into the car beside the Vice President and pulled at the seat belt strap.

"I wish everybody would do that, use their seat belts I mean, it would save a lot of misery. Raffi is a very good driver but there are some real idiots about. I think we take our lives into our hands every time we get into a car in this country. Don't you agree? Do you know that we've officially had a driving test for over forty years but most people simply buy their licences on the black market or get someone else to take the test for them? It's a disgrace. Would you like a sherbet lemon? They're English, a sweetie; I'm totally addicted to them. The trick is to suck it without crunching it for as long as possible. Then finally, on the inside, there is some splendidly fizzy sherbet."

Nasir took a sweet from the bag. He concentrated on not crunching it and said nothing. The Vice President's words had immediately stirred the difficult memories of his parents' death, not that long ago, in a traffic accident. He hadn't a clue what to say anyway but all sorts of things were going through his mind. It came to him that he was indeed taking his life into his hands in more ways than one by accepting the lift. The sherbet came as a tangy surprise. He could see why the Vice President liked them so much.

The Vice President of the Republic was Saali al-Malimi. He had been Vice President for almost as long as the President had been in power and that was over twenty years. He was also the country's Foreign Minister, its smiling face at the U.N., its benign presence abroad. The bond between President and Vice President was not in doubt. Other ministers rarely lasted more than two or three years, being shuffled around from one post to another and promoted or demoted almost seemingly at random. Others came and went, Saali remained.

Opinion was divided about Saali al-Malimi, at home and abroad. To some people he was the acceptable face of the Regime, untainted by scandal or by personal implication in the many excessive violations of human rights that had occurred over the years. He was an intellectual, a linguist educated at the Sorbonne, and a published poet besides. He was mild mannered, polite, never losing his temper, always ready to face the international press and answer questions, however difficult. He'd even had an audience with the Pope. He could be trusted. To others he was the 'crafty one', the President's trustee, slippery, manipulative and deliberately put forward as a moderate front man to mask the reality of the Regime. How else could he have managed to maintain his position over all those long years? There was another view too, that al-Malimi remained as Vice President simply because he had never become a threat, a rival, a challenge to the President. He had no position in the ruling Party and no followers, Party or otherwise. He didn't have a military background, no loyal regiments behind him. He wasn't linked to any cliques. He hadn't used his position to further and entrench the interests of his family; in fact he had no family to speak of. He lived modestly with his two unmarried sisters, had never married and had no sons or daughters to follow in his footsteps. Saali al-Malimi was, according to this viewpoint, a non-entity, a lackey despatched here and there to do the President's bidding.

"You mentioned English lessons?" asked Nasir, as a way of breaking the silence.

"Ah yes,' came the reply, 'my great niece, at least I think that's what she is, I'm not very good at genealogy. Anyway, she's ten years old and they live in the Zone. Her father is the manager of one of the hotels there. A very bright girl. We should arrive much earlier than you would have done on the bus, so I'll take you there to begin with, if that's all right."

Nasir was still wary. It was a strange way to arrange tuition.

"I don't understand this. If you want me to give English lessons, why not just call me on the phone? Why follow me and pick me up on the street? It doesn't add up."

"Well, let me be frank Mr Raziq, I expect that your phone is monitored and you do have history. It wouldn't look good for me to be associated with a known dissident, however tenuously. I could have got someone else to contact you but you come highly recommended and I wanted to meet you in person. And yes, we were following you but actually we were following you for quite some time before you spotted us. I needed to be sure that no one else was following you too. It wouldn't do to have our meeting reported. And it isn't just about English lessons. I really do want to have a conversation with you about certain matters but we can do that a little later. Now please sit back and enjoy the journey. I expect it's a lot more comfortable than the bus. Would you like another sweetie?"

Within a few minutes they were leaving the dusty outskirts of the capital and into the dry, barren countryside. As you might expect for North Africa it was flat, sandy and almost featureless. Sometimes you could see for miles but on this day the wind was up and the sky was full of dust. Through the darkened side windows Nasir could see nothing at all. Visibility through the windscreen wasn't much better. The industrial park of the Special Zone appeared suddenly, out of the gloom. It was enclosed within high barbed wire fences, with a single entrance and exit. Goods made inside were intended only for export and vehicles leaving were subject to thorough searches to prevent those goods entering the domestic economy and undercutting local prices. The tourist area, a bit further on, was also enclosed within wire fencing but this was fronted with abundant and well-watered planting, especially poincianas and climbing bougainvillea. The effect was quite lovely. The guards at the main entrance motioned to the car to halt but allowed it through without stopping, once they recognised Raffi.

Inside it was like entering a different country. Everywhere was green, the terrain landscaped to give rises and hollows, all planted with grass, palm trees and other exotic types of vegetation. Even the tarmac on the road was smooth and pristine. They drove through a golf course, electric buggies on either side, the greens cut to perfection. Further on, before the hotels and the seafront, they passed clusters of villas, each one architect designed, each villa with its own swimming pool, some with more than one. Of course, it wasn't Nasir's first visit but each one he made caused mixed emotions. Part of him was envious of those people who lived or worked there, envious of the environment. How good it would be to live in that sort of luxury, to have his son grow up there. But it was disturbing too because Nasir knew that much of the wealth on show was the product of corruption and he felt contempt for people who lived in such conditions when just a few miles away the realities of life were so very different.

The car pulled up at the front gates of a particularly grand villa. Raffi opened his side window, pressed an electronic key to the reader and the gates opened. So did the huge door to the garage further on. Raffi drove in, stopped and then got out to open the Vice President's door. Raffi handed Saali a walking stick and helped him out. Saali moved slowly, using the stick for support, his body stooped. Nasir hadn't really looked at him since that first glance of recognition but there, in the garage, he saw a very different image to the one displayed on posters, in the press and on television. That Saali was smooth, vibrant, almost ageless. The real thing was aged, the face lined and the body slightly bent. Nasir also noticed a hearing aid.

The housekeeper was waiting at the door. As the Vice President approached she started to curtsy.

"Oh stop all that you old fool, Hatti,' said Saali affectionately. 'Tell the others we're here and bring me a cold beer. One for you Mr Raziq?"

"I don't...."

"Oh yes, a good Muslim, of course. I'm afraid I have to confess to a few weaknesses but to tell you the truth, at my age I'm beyond bothering about the consequences. An orange juice then Hatti, for our guest and have cook prepare some food for Raffi. You know how much he loves her cooking."

Saali led the way through to the lounge. It was very spacious, furnished with three big sofas and various tables, rugs and exotic pot plants. It opened onto a large patio and beyond that the pool. A lady, wearing only a swim suit that was cut high at the sides and low at the front, got up from a lounger and came towards them, body glistening.

"This is Mr Raziq,' said Saali, not bothering with any of the usual formalities. 'You were told to expect him?"

"Of course. Hello Mr Raziq, pleased to meet you. I'm Samira," she said, smiling and holding out her hand.

Nasir felt very uncomfortable. He was not used to women wearing so little. He shook her hand, hardly gripping it at all and desperately sought the right words.

"Your daughter wants English lessons?"

"Oh goodness, she's not my daughter,' said Samira, still smiling and glancing down at herself, 'I don't look that old, do I? I'm just the nanny. Yasmin's parents aren't here right now. They're in Paris for a tourism convention. I'll fetch her for you. She's online at the moment."

Samira went off as Hatti arrived with the drinks.

"It's a lovely place, don't you think?' enquired Saali. 'Mind you, some people would find it almost decadent. For myself, I prefer to live more simply in the capital, in the real world. Yasmin's my great niece on my late brother's side. Don't worry; he made his money legitimately, in business in America. I try to stay close to them all, no kids myself, never married, never found a woman who could put up with me, in fact. Samira's a real beauty, don't you think?"

Nasir took it as a rhetorical question and sipped his orange juice. Presently Samira came back with Yasmin. The girl was tall for her age, almost as tall as Nasir. After the introductions he asked her why she wanted to learn English.

"To be able to read Harry Potter in its original language. I get the impression that a lot gets lost in translation."

Saali raised his eyes and his eyebrows and gave an exasperated look.

"I told you she was bright."

The arrangements were quickly made. Nasir was to come two times a week in the early evening when school was finished. Saali offered payment in euros (all the establishments in the Special Zone accepted payment in euros, as well as local currency), saying that they could be exchanged for much more than the official rate, but Nasir declined, fearing a trap. Illegal money dealing was punishable by imprisonment, and he did not want to provide the authorities with an excuse for picking him up.

"I'm afraid you'll have to make your own way here but we may be able to fix you up with something instead of the bus. The bus takes ages. I'll see what I can do."

Very soon Yasmin went back to her room and Samira to her sunbathing. Nasir and Saali were left alone in the room. Saali beckoned him to sit on one of the sofas and then sat down on one adjacent. Nasir felt awkward. He wondered what was coming next.

"Tell me, Nasir, you don't mind if I call you Nasir do you, we don't need to be formal? The President is getting on. He can't live forever. What do you hope for when he is gone?"

The question took Nasir aback. It was the last sort of thing he was expecting. The slight feeling of panic returned. How should he answer? Was it a trap? Did he really want his true opinion and what if he gave it? Eventually he decided to take a chance.

"I hope this country can gradually move towards a liberal democracy. Free elections, an end to censorship, a proper system of justice, land and wealth redistribution, that sort of thing."

"And do you think that this is what will actually happen when the President is gone?"

Once again Nasir decided to be bold.

"Almost certainly not. The President's son will succeed him. Everybody knows that. Nothing will change. It may even get worse...... Look, why are you asking me these sorts of questions? You said I had history. What did you mean? You're making me feel very uncomfortable. People aren't allowed to talk about this kind of thing."

Saali smiled.

"I'm sorry. I know this must be difficult. I have made it my business to find out about you. Yes, I do know about your history. You spent two days in No 42 about ten years ago, a trivial matter, student bravado. No charges were brought. It was a warning, that's all, but after that your movements were monitored. It was observed that some of your acquaintances held dissident views. One of your university colleagues reported you for making unacceptable statements, admittedly in private, and due to this your room was raided and things removed but, once again, no charges were brought. You come from a rural village, way out in the heartland. Your parents were peasants but your father owned and farmed a few acres so he was of some standing locally. Somehow he struggled to put you through school. You are married. Your wife is very different to you, very conservative in her views, wears the veil. I expect it was arranged. You have a son, about four years old. Since the university has been closed you have made a meagre living through translation and English lessons. I know all this about you and something more besides. You interest me. Tell me Nasir do you believe that the university was closed because of the discovery of a terrorist plot?"

Again, Nasir had not anticipated that sort of question. He paused before answering, trying to decide whether to follow the official line or tell the truth. Once more he decided to be brave.

"No, of course not. It was the start of the Arab Spring, the uprisings. Things were kicking off all over the place. Students were always at the forefront of the demonstrations, so the university was closed to prevent that from happening. That is why it remains closed."

"Quite right Nasir, that is correct. The Al-Qaeda plot

was just an excuse, and if you remember, it was about the same time that two other important things happened. Structural defects were discovered in our two great central mosques that necessitated their closure. Of course there are plenty of other mosques but these are much smaller, away from the centre. Friday prayers is always a dangerous time. Demonstrations are banned, meetings have to be approved but we can do nothing about Friday prayers, nothing to stop men gathering for that. So, from our point of view, it's better if there are a number of smaller gatherings in the outlying districts, rather than one or two big ones in the centre. And then there were the archaeological excavations that necessitated the closure of Independence Square. That was my idea."

"To prevent another Tahrir Square?"

"No, no, no. Not to prevent a Tahrir Square but to avert another Tiananmen Square. The Minister of the Interior would have had no hesitation in sending in tanks if he thought the Regime was threatened. He is completely ruthless, without scruples. That is what I sought to prevent, to prevent the senseless massacre of ordinary, decent people. You may think that I am an ogre, Mr Raziq, the spokesman of the Regime as some say, but I assure you that I have always tried to strive for moderation. When I studied the events elsewhere, in Egypt, Tunisia etc, certain common factors were apparent. Students were always prominent. They may not have provided the initial spark but they were quickly involved. The uprisings were not top led, prominent politicians were initially wary of becoming involved but students took up the call. Friday prayers always provided the opportunity to gather, to demonstrate deeply held frustrations, but also to incite. Finally, there was almost always a focal point, a rallying place where people could gather, be it Tahrir Square or even some roundabout on the ring road, but somewhere that could become the focus."

Saali paused, finished his beer and called out to Hatti to bring him another and more orange juice for Nasir too.

"You see Nasir, you see what's happened elsewhere? Chaos in Libya, civil war in Syria and reversion to military dictatorship in Egypt, because that's what it is, even if the president there is now technically a civilian. And everywhere the salafists are making ground. Isis declaring a caliphate and committing unspeakable atrocities in Syria and Iraq, terrorism in sub-Saharan Africa, Pakistan and who knows where else. And all of it entirely predictable. You say that you would like to see a liberal democracy but that just isn't going to happen in this part of the world. We have no experience of democracy, only of dictatorship, be it repressive or benign. History shows that you can't make a simple transition from dictatorship to democracy. There are too many vested interests to overcome, too many people with secrets to protect and axes to grind. And there are other forces to consider. The Brotherhood is here too. Out in the villages and the small towns, it is the Brotherhood that calls the tune. Not openly, of course, but we know how strong they are. Give them the opportunity through free elections and they will take it. They will sound moderate to begin with, while the foreign media are focussed on them, but once in power, well you saw what Morsi was like in Egypt, to know what it will be like if they come to power here too."

Hatti came in with more drinks. Saali waited until she had left before continuing.

"I am worried about this country Mr Raziq. Very worried about what will happen when the President is gone. I am going to let you into a secret Mr Raziq, a very big secret indeed. The President is dying. Yes, President Baashir is dying. He is in the advanced stages of stomach cancer and has only a few months, at best, left. Nothing can be done. It is inoperable. Chemotherapy has postponed the inevitable but the best specialists are in agreement. A few months, maybe three, at most."

There was a silence. Saali seemed to be waiting for Nasir to respond but Nasir had no idea what to say. Half of him was shocked that the President might soon be dead but alarm bells were also ringing. Was it the truth or was it a lie, a device to trap him, to give himself away? Saali must know about the blog. That was the only explanation. That was why he had been picked up in the street; that was why he was here. The Vice President must know that he was behind the blog.

"Have you nothing to say, Mr Raziq? Aren't you shocked at such terrible news? Then again maybe, perhaps it rather pleases you? Come now, Mr Raziq, you must say something."

"I don't know what to say. I only know that I don't know why you are telling me this. I am a nobody. I earn barely enough to keep my family fed. I have no power or influence and I am a total stranger to you, so why are you telling me this? I don't understand it. You must have me here for a reason. It can't just be about English lessons. If it's true that the President has cancer, why would you tell me? I think I need an answer now or I'm just going to get up and leave."

Saali paused for a few seconds, took another sip of his drink, and then continued. Once again, it was not what Nasir expected.

"We grew up together, you know, Baashir and I, as youngsters. He doesn't like to talk about his childhood because they were so very poor, so not much has been written. My father was a businessman, in the export, import trade. There were lots of opportunities at that time, after the war, so he made money fast. Drove a flashy American car, a Thunderbird, as I remember, you know, one of the ones that had those enormous tail fins. We had this big place, a mansion really, and there was this little empty plot of land next to us, and one day he picked me up from school and we drove home, and there they were, trying to cobble together some sort of shelter from wood and metal sheets and cardboard. My mother was horrified. She wanted my dad to get them moved on but he thought they might only be temporary and I think he felt sorry for them. His father had this ramshackle cart and every day he must have walked miles with it to all the various souks and markets, picking up stuff, delivering, earning a pittance. There were six children. His mother was around thirty but looked much older. He was my age almost exactly, birthdays in the same month, and we got on like a house on fire. You couldn't keep us apart. My mother forbade me from going there, she was a bit snobbish about them, Shias as well, but I went anyway, whenever I could. In time his mum built this clay oven outside in the yard and every day she baked bread and the smell of it was wonderful. We would sit by it and wait till the bread was done, and she would take one and break bits off for us, so hot you couldn't hold onto them.

My mother hated me playing with him but my dad was more pragmatic. He had an 'if you can't beat them, join them' sort of attitude, so first of all he got the father a regular job in one of his warehouses, and then he offered to pay for Baashir to attend the same school as me. Of course, he was way behind in things like writing and spelling and maths but, my word, was he clever. He caught up so quickly, and pretty soon he was top of the class. If anything that made my mother even more angry.

Saali paused at this point. His eyes seemed to be watering, as if his words had stirred cherished memories. Nasir wanted him to continue. It was fascinating to learn about the President's past.

"Go on please; it's all new to me. I didn't know."

"Well, when it came to the end of school days, I wanted to go to university in Cairo. Ever since Nasser it was the place to be but my father would have none of it. The Sorbonne, Paris or nothing, he told me and so, like the good son I was, I applied there and was accepted. Baashir was almost one of the family by then and Dad would have paid for him as well but Baashir had only one thought in his mind, the army. Even I was horrified. The army was detested as the instrument of foreign control. Most of the officer class were French and those that weren't were seen as lackeys, collaborators who were only officers because they'd bought their commissions. The ordinary soldiers were basically just peasants. Most were illiterate. Only a few were educated even to end of primary standard. My father told him he was wasting himself after all the money that he had spent on him over the years but Baashir was insistent. When my father asked him why he just said that he thought he was cut out for a military life. With me he was more forthcoming.

"Look Saali," he said, "you will become an academic, write books, maybe become famous that way. My ambitions are different. The colonial tide is turning. The days of French rule are numbered. Already there is talk of a monarchy. And once the French pull out they will take their officers with them. Who will fill their shoes? Mark my words, Saali, then the army will need people like me, people who are educated and clever. Within a few years I will be an officer, and a few years later I intend to be Commander in Chief, and you and I both know that whoever commands the army, runs the country. The pattern has been set in Egypt. It will be the same here. This will become a republic and I will be its first president. Then there will be some changes, real changes.

He was quite serious, no joke. He had it all worked out. I remember thinking that he'd gone mad but then history has shown that his assessment of the situation was entirely correct. So, at the same time as I went off to Paris, Baashir enlisted. Not as an officer, you understand, but at the very bottom, a private. Within two years, at the age of twenty no less, he was a sergeant and when the French pulled out and their officers left, they needed officers fast and, of course, with his ability and his education, he was an obvious choice. So he was commissioned and then rapidly promoted. A colonel before the age of thirty, and you know the rest."

Nasir looked at his watch. He would have to leave soon if he was not to be late for the lesson. Saali understood.

"Couldn't you message, say you'll be a bit late, make an excuse, there's more to say, more I need to talk to you about?"

Nasir looked at him, the man he had thought a nonentity, the President's lapdog. He'd always felt hatred and contempt towards him, but this Saali was rather charming, almost vulnerable in the way he was opening up. Besides, how could he go and not know why he had been summoned, whether he was in danger, what the Vice President had in store for him? Of course he had to stay. Nasir took out his phone and sent the text.

"I can stay for another thirty minutes Mr Vice President. Tell me why I am here."

Once again Saali ignored the question.

"He was full of good intentions at the start, a health care system, free primary schooling for all. We used to spend hours talking about how the country would be transformed into a modern secular state, and I believe it could have happened had it not been for her."

Saali didn't have to name 'her'. Nasir knew who he was talking about, the First Lady of the Republic, the President's second wife. Basma had been a typist working in the Ministry of Defence, when she met the President, although he was still an army officer at the time. The President's first marriage had been an arranged one but happy. Mia had presented him with a daughter after a year but had nearly died in the process. After she had recovered it was in the knowledge that there would be no more children.

"I'll let you into another little secret Nasir, I detest the First Lady. Yes, it's true, I really detest her. She was a nobody with ideas above her station when he met her and she inveigled her way into his affections. Basma knew that she would be able to provide the one thing that Mia could not and that was a son. That's how she snared him. There was a rumour, I don't know whether it was true or not but I wouldn't be surprised if it was, that she had already become pregnant by him but got rid of it because it was a girl. Anyway being able to give him a son was the key. In this society people want boys first and Baashir was no exception, so when Basma became pregnant and the test confirmed it was a boy, he divorced Mia and married her. I'm sorry; you probably know all this already. I'm coming to the crux of the matter now. I have a reputation for loyalty but my loyalty is to the President and that is as far as it extends. We are a republic and presidents should be elected. I don't like dynasties and I particularly don't want to see this country dominated by that woman and her extended family. In other words I don't want to see Chafik step into the presidency when his father dies."

"And what has this got to do with me? You still haven't told me why I am here."

"My contacts tell me that you are the person behind the blog 'The People Demand the End of the Regime'."

The words felt almost like bullets to Nasir, even though he had guessed it must be something to do with the blog.

"I don't know what you're talking about."

"Come now, my friend, do you think that I wouldn't have checked and double checked. You are one of the authors and that is why you are here. I have a proposal to put to you. You look alarmed. That is entirely natural. You know that if the security forces were to identify you, you would be locked away in a cell and left to rot, but only after you had been tortured to extract the other names. Actually, that is probably not true. After you had been tortured you would almost certainly be executed. But the point is that the security forces do not know about you, only me, only I, Saali, only I know about you, and I am not going to tell them, so you can relax, I assure you. You are in no danger from me."

The words did not have their intended effect. He felt frightened and vulnerable.

"I have nothing to do with that blog. I am leaving now, this is just ridiculous."

"Please calm yourself. Really, you are in no danger. You are here because of the blog and I am talking to you because I want to help you make the blog even more interesting by giving you information that will be even more damaging to the Regime, information which you would never otherwise find out about. Now that's a proposal Nasir, isn't it, a proposal with a capital P. I want to feed you with information to put on the blog. I want you to use it to prevent the accession of Chafik."

Nasir had broken out into a sweat by this time. His mind was racing. He felt a sense of panic. This man, who had the power to have him taken away and executed, this man knew all about it. In his mind images of his son, his parents, flashed before him. He saw the cell where he had been taken previously, felt the leather thong on his back and soles, imagined the hangman's noose placed around his neck. Every instinct told him to deny, to get away. Nasir stood up and started to leave.

"I told you, I have nothing to do with the blog."

The Vice President just sat there, calm and composed.

"Very well, Nasir, let me explain how I know. Please sit down again. If you don't want to help me after you hear what I have to say, then you can leave and your secret will be safe with me."

Nasir was not reassured at all but he sat down.

"This is what I have established, Nasir. We know that the blog must be posted abroad because we are very good at controlling domestic internet traffic. We can block the sites, even isolate the devices that are used, but with this blog we can't because it comes from abroad. Your blog is very popular, Nasir. It is seen by many thousands of people, here and abroad. It tells the world of things the authorities would rather be kept hidden, who has been arrested, instances of corruption, graffiti that indicates internal opposition. In other words, it is a thorn, and they have been trying to find out who is responsible, so that it can be plucked out and destroyed. In this they have drawn a blank. After all, the number of potential suspects who have to be investigated runs into many thousands. Just look at the number of arrests that have been made in the last decade alone, and all of them persons with a reason to hold a grudge and get involved.

"Because I was interested in this blog and because the authorities had got nowhere, I decided to try a different approach. Knowing that the blog was posted abroad, I began to wonder how it got there. It could not have been through a call that relayed the information, because at some point it would have been intercepted. It could not have been sent through the mail because that would take too long. Some of the information on the blog was there too soon after it had happened, for it to have been sent that way. So I came to the conclusion that someone must have taken the information abroad and posted it on the internet there, and the most obvious, indeed the only possible way, given the speed with which the information was posted, must be by air. Now your blog is always posted on a Thursday, in the afternoon, in fact, so I had my people check out all the regular Thursday morning flights from the international airport. We trawled through the list of destinations, pilots, flight crews and passengers, and we found a few likely candidates, but when we investigated further, they were all ruled out. Then, a few weeks ago, there was a week when the blog did not appear. It was there as usual the following week but absent that week and that absence was crucial. Once again we looked at the sequence of flights, to see if there was a regular one that hadn't been scheduled or which, for some reason, hadn't gone ahead, but we drew another blank. Then I had another little thought; perhaps we had been looking in the wrong place. What about the airport in the Special Zone? This time we were successful. Every Thursday a private jet flies to Malta in the morning and returns in the early evening. A few weeks ago it didn't. There was a gap. The flight was scheduled but cancelled. This flight has only three regular occupants, the pilot, Madame Bouvainne and her personal assistant. Madame Bouvainne is, of course, a pillar of the establishment. She flies to Malta every Thursday to visit her aged mother, and to play bridge. It could not possibly be her. That left her secretary and the pilot. That's when we found out. Madame Bouvainne's secretary has a history that coincides with your own, Nasir. She was also a student at the university who was briefly detained for taking part in the same demonstration that led to your own detention.

"Of course, in finding this out, I had her followed and guess what, every Wednesday afternoon, which incidentally is her afternoon off, she goes to a particular café for tea and cake and there she meets a man who stays only a few minutes but who is observed to pass her a small object which I can only surmise to be a memory stick. There, you have it Nasir. You give her the memory stick, and she takes it to Malta, and while Madame Bouvainne is playing bridge she uploads the blog onto the internet."

The Vice President sat back and finished his second beer. Nasir felt the panic of entrapment. There was nothing he could do. Saali knew everything. There was no point in denial.

"Of course, once we had made the link with the secretary, we also investigated the other students who took part in that little protest. I think you know where I'm leading Nasir. I know all about you, and all your fellow conspirators. But please be aware of this, I have known this information for several weeks and all of you are still free. None have been taken in. The blog still appears. Surely you must realise that I am sincere when I say that you are in no danger from me. If you were, I could have had you all arrested some time past. I really do want you and your blog to enable me to discredit the Regime. Not the President personally but those who stand to assume power when he is gone. This is what I propose Nasir. For the moment I would prefer if you didn't publicise the President's illness. That can come later. For now I want you to start with Chafik."

Saali reached into a pocket, took out an envelope and handed it to Nasir.

"Another memory stick. I'm sure you will find the contents interesting. All of it is completely true, I assure you. I expect to read all about it on your blog. Don't put it all out at once. Over a few weeks would be better, to build up the interest. Take very great care please. Once any of this gets out they will redouble, quadruple, their efforts to uncover who is responsible. We should not meet again. It is important to be careful. Samira will be our go between. Make use of her, Nasir. She will pass on more revelations, and she will tell you when to make public the President's illness. Your blog is going to go through the roof because of this and one day it might make you famous but for now you must keep a very low profile. You must understand, however, that if you are discovered and implicate me, I shall deny any involvement. Do not mention me to any of your contacts either. No one else should know about this."

Without waiting for Nasir to respond the Vice President called out for Samira and Raffi.

"I have to get back to the capital. Samira will take you to your lesson. Are we agreed on the way ahead? Will you help me?"

Saali held out his hand. Nasir, having no real idea of what to say, shook it briefly.

"Good, I thought I could count on you, Nasir. I know this must have been difficult for you, alarming even, but you really do have the chance now to do something of immense importance for your country. We may not meet again, who knows, but I thank you."

As Saali left the room, Samira came in, wearing a T shirt over her swimming costume and with trainers on her feet.

"Come along now, Nasir, let's get you to your lesson."

The next hour or so went by in a blur. Somehow Nasir taught his lesson but all the while his mind was on what had happened. When the lesson was finished and he stepped outside there was another surprise, a car was waiting, with Samira and Yasmin inside. The side window wound down.

"Can we offer you a lift, Nasir? We're off to do some shopping in the capital. You might as well hop in. Yasmin, pop into the back so that Mr Raziq and I can talk."

Nasir was relieved that Samira was fully dressed. It had been a bit disconcerting sitting next to her on the way to the lesson. This time she was in slacks and a tunic and her hair was hidden by a hijab.

"How did the lesson go, Mr Raziq?"

"To tell you the truth, I'm not quite sure. My talk with the Vice President was so unexpected that it was difficult for me to concentrate on it."

They said nothing more for the next few minutes until Yasmin turned on her music player and put on her headphones.

"It's better to drive you home like this. No chance of you getting picked up, especially with what you're carrying. He's a good man, you know, Saali. You can trust him. I've known him all my life. He has explained the situation to me and the part I have to play. I will do whatever he asks and willingly. You have nothing to fear from him."

Nasir didn't reply. He was searching for words but none came. It was such a strange situation. Samira was silent too for most of the journey and it was only as they entered the city and headed towards the warren of streets where he lived, that she spoke again.

"I have a flat here in the city. I'm there at weekends. Her parents always come home for the weekends. This is my mobile number. Call me if you need to. You could come over."

With that she passed him a scrap of paper, and Nasir felt her hand briefly clasp his.

Nasir asked to be dropped off some blocks away from where he lived. District Eight was one of the capital's poorest areas. Since he'd moved in with his family he had always felt slightly ashamed to be living there and he wondered what his new pupil and Samira would think if they saw what it was like. District Eight certainly was very neglected, the streets were full of potholes, there were no pavements and the traffic threw up clouds of dust. In places the stench of raw sewage permeated the air. Bunches of electricity cables, like black spaghetti, hung almost haphazardly from wooden poles and lined the streets. The previous week a child had been electrocuted when the metal rod she had been carrying, had touched one of the wires. Most of the housing was jerry built after the Second World War for people drawn from the countryside seeking work and at a time when there were no building regulations or minimum standards. Nasir's home was a two storey building shabbily made of breeze blocks, with four small rooms and a toilet in the back yard. At least it had running water and electricity. Some of the housing there didn't even have that. When it rained, admittedly not often, the roof leaked. Nasir had been trying to save up to afford something better in a different neighbourhood. The closure of the university had put paid to that. Some weeks now he struggled to afford the rent.

It was only after the rest of the family were in bed that Nasir brought out the small tablet that he kept hidden, even from his wife. He plugged in the memory stick and was deeply shocked by its contents. The President's eldest son, Chafik, was shown to have been involved in various deceptions and scandals, none of which had ever been made public. Nasir realised that the material he was reading could have a potentially explosive impact on public opinion if it were leaked, and yet that was what he was being expected to do. He also realised that in doing so he would be putting his life in real danger. Once the first new entry into the blog had been made the authorities would stop at nothing to discover its author. Nasir thought about all the other people who contributed to or knew about the blog, so many people who would be in danger or who might give him away were any of them to be taken in and tortured.

Later, after having replaced the tablet, complete with the memory stick, in its hiding place, Nasir tried to go over the day's events in order to try to decide what he should do. Among the many thoughts he had were suspicions of the Vice President's motives. Constitutionally he was next in line if the President were to die in office but everybody knew that the President's intended successor was Chafik, so was he, Nasir, merely being used as a pawn to further Saali's own political ambitions, a pawn furthermore, who could be discarded and thrown to the wolves once he had served his purpose? Yet, if the contents of the stick were actually true, then it would be a disaster if Chafik were to succeed his father, so maybe Saali's intentions were honourable. Then there was Samira. What was her part? He could understand her giving him her number, but 'You could come over', that stuck in his mind, as did Saali's invitation to 'make use of her'. Was she just the proverbial bait to string him along?

TWO

SAALI AL-MALIMI WAS in an excellent frame of mind as Raafi drove him to his meeting with the President. Nasir had done a good job in gradually releasing the information he had been given, and it was having its intended effect. First of all there was the revelation that Chafik, who held the rank of General in the National Army (although he was not officially attached to any unit), had twice failed the exams in the first American military academy in which he had been enrolled, and had been sent down. Then there was the disclosure that he had then been expelled from the second academy, having been found in a compromising position with the Principal's wife. Next, the two fatal car crashes in Europe (Chafik's love of fast cars was well known), that had resulted in arrest and charges of causing death through dangerous driving. There were the enormous sums that Chafik had lost and won in various casinos and the photos of him, drunken and dishevelled, and with women, provocatively dressed, some of whom were identified as prostitutes. There was more. Chafik had shot and killed a man during an argument in a nightclub in Nice. He had spent time in a rehab unit in California for cocaine addiction. He and two brothers of the President's wife, had had enormous villas built for themselves in the Special Zone, using aid money donated by France to fund medical units in rural areas, this having resulted in the temporary suspension of French aid. None of this was public knowledge and none of the various charges that had been brought against Chafik in the various countries where he had offended, had been taken further, because care was always taken to arrange diplomatic credentials and therefore immunity, in advance.

The presidential palace, to which Saali was being driven, was an impressively long, white, two-storey building, with a large dome at its centre. Set within manicured grounds, it was encircled by a low wall, topped by elaborate wrought iron fencing and razor wire. Saali occasionally used the main gates where he would acknowledge the recognition of the crowd that was always gathered, but this time he instructed Raafi to drive round to the rear deliveries entrance. Once inside, he walked directly to the President's private offices and waited to be called. The President, Baashir al-Baqri, Guardian of the Revolution, Father of the Nation and Champion of the Oppressed, to name but a few of his official titles he had awarded himself, looked surprisingly well. He smiled and rose from his seat as Saali entered and walked towards him quite easily with just the aid of a cane. They embraced warmly.

"You look so much better today."

"The doctors are pleased. Maybe it's the start of remission or maybe it's the drugs they've just pumped into me, but yes, I am better today. Yesterday was terrible. Come, will you walk me round the garden? You know I like to get a bit of exercise at least once a day."

Outside they felt able to talk more freely, although Saali had once wondered whether the very trees might have been planted with listening devices. He unwrapped and handed the President a sweet. It was part of a routine; he knew how much he liked them.

"Have you discovered anything?" asked Baashir.

"Nothing at all. Whoever is behind this blog is being very careful. I've not got any leads. Surely the Minister of the Interior has come up with something."

"As of this morning I have no Minister of the Interior. Useless fool. Will you take up the position? At least I would know that you would be doing your best."

"My hands are full already. In any case you know that I'm not cut out for that sort of role. There must be someone else."

"She suspects you, you know."

"What?"

"That you're behind it. Basma suspects you; she says that you will be the one to benefit most if Chafik does not succeed me."

"Preposterous. You know I have never wanted to be president. I never really wanted to be involved in politics at all, until you asked me."

"She also says that you are one of the few people to be party to all the unfortunate information that's come out. She's quite made up her mind."

"Surely you can't..."

"Relax, my friend, my very dear friend. I know it isn't you. I have complete confidence that you would never betray me. It's a warning, a warning that's all, a warning to be careful about her. She's never liked you. We both know that. She's always resented the friendship we have, that we go back together much further than her. Last week she asked me to get rid of you. No, not literally, not in that way, but to appoint her brother as Vice President in your place. When I refused she flew into such a rage as I've never seen before. Such words, such obscenities. She is becoming desperate. All this stuff coming out about Chafik has really got to her. She knows that it makes it very difficult for him to succeed me, at least in the short run anyway. And you are an obstacle to that as well because constitutionally, you are next in line. That is why you need to be careful. She will do anything and everything to secure Chafik's place and you know how powerful she is."

Saali let him talk. He had never heard him talk like this about Basma before. The President paused though, leaning heavily on his stick, his face perspiring from the heat of the day and grimacing from the effort of walking and maybe from the burden of his thoughts.

"I know how many times you've tried to warn me about her. To tell you the truth I used to think it was a sort of jealousy on your part, that you were offended that she had somehow come between us. It's only come gradually, the realisation that there was some truth in what you were saying. Perhaps it's only natural though, after all the position of First Lady is one of high status, and she has had to take on more and more as my illness has progressed. And let's face it, this is a difficult time for her, my cancer, the blog about Chafik, she's bound to be on edge. But do be careful, there's no knowing how she will react, what her plans are, after I'm gone."

Saali said nothing and they walked on slowly and in silence, for a few minutes, but he was thinking of how little his friend actually knew about Basma, of her indiscretions with other men, even of her procurement of suitable women, young girls really, to satisfy the President's lust. Or the secret bank accounts, stuffed with payments from local and international businessmen, in return for lucrative contracts. Perhaps the time had come for Nasir's blog to shift its focus away from Chafik and onto the President's wife.

"You know, I sometimes wonder if it has all been worth it."

The President's words interrupted Saali's train of thought.

"Worth it?"

"Remember when we were young, before all this, when we used to talk about how we would transform this country. I wonder what happened to the person I was then?"

Saali did not say what he thought, that the President had become intoxicated with the trappings, no, not with the trappings of power, but with power itself. That he had chosen tyranny above benevolence.

"But look at this country, how strong it is now compared to how decrepit and corrupt it was before you took over."

"Perhaps that is true. This country stands alone now. The French, the Russians, the Americans, nobody controls us any more, nobody tells us, tells me, what to do. That will be my legacy for people to look up to when I am..."

The President's words went unfinished. Saali knew that he was thinking about the cancer and said nothing.

"Mia?" asked the President. It was a question he asked very occasionally.

"She's fine, as always. Still in Paris. I saw her last week. She always asks about you but I haven't told her about the illness yet."

"And the girl?"

Saali wondered why he could never bring himself to use her name. Perhaps it was guilt.

"Girl? Come now, she's nearly thirty. A beautiful, talented woman, not a girl. I haven't seen her in Paris for some time. She travels a lot. No husband yet, though I daresay there have been several suitors. Don't worry, everything is taken care of. Neither of them will want for anything and they are both safe.'

Saali was tempted to say that 'she' would never find them but thought better of it.

"Now, you are looking tired. Let me help you back inside."

Saali took the President's arm and escorted him back to his private apartment. On the way he broached the subject of the university.

"I have been thinking, the Arab Spring is well and truly over and the risk of an uprising here with it. Now would be a good time to reopen the university, don't you think? We really do need to be producing graduates if this country is to develop. Quite a few of the staff have already accepted positions elsewhere, and we don't want to lose any more. It would also show that we feel secure and confident. Now would be a good time."

"Instruct the Minister of Education to see to it," was the President's response.

On his way out he found one of Basma's equerries waiting and was asked to go her quarters. Saali knew that refusal was not really an option, and that he would be required to wait before she made her appearance. When she did, she entered the room as elegantly groomed as ever, although Saali found so much make-up on a woman of her age, slightly absurd. Basma greeted him with the usual false charm, saying how good it was to see him, how young he continued to look, and did he have some secret elixir of youth that he could share with her. Saali had heard it all before but responded as expected. Tea and sweetmeats were brought and consumed, Saali commented on the lightness of the pastry, knowing that the real business of the day would only start when she decided. He also anticipated that the blog, and his own position as Vice President, would be at the top of her agenda. He was correct.

"This business of the, what do you call it, a blog, this blog thing on the internet about Chafik, you must realise that it's having a terrible effect on the President. He has enough to worry about anyway with the illness, without this. Have you not got any idea about who may be responsible?"

"Madam,' he always addressed her as 'Madam', it was expected, 'Madam, he has his best security people onto it. If they haven't been able to find out who is behind it, then there is no point in asking me. It isn't my sort of area. I have no expertise."

"Well, that maybe so but what is obvious to both of us is that this business is designed to undermine Chafik's position as next in line. The President's mind would be put at rest if he could be sure about what is going to happen when the cancer finally gets the better of him. Have you not considered giving up the vice presidency in favour of Chafik? That would show the nation our confidence in him, despite all this silliness."

"Madam, of course I have considered it but we both realise that my first duty is to the President and I can do no such thing until he requests it of me."

"Come now, Saali, you don't need his agreement or permission to resign the post. You could do that anyway and it would make the transfer of power so much smoother if his successor is in place when he does die."

"Yes, Madam, it's true that I don't need his permission, but I do need to have his approval. I have talked about it with him and it is clear to me that he does not want this now, not until this business of Chafik has blown over. I am sorry, Madam, but we must have patience in this matter. The President knows best."

Saali could see the agitation in her face.

"You know there are those who suspect that you are part of this conspiracy to discredit Chafik. What do you say to that?"

"Madam, I know that some people could interpret it in that way. I am the Vice President. If Chafik is excluded then that position is strengthened but you know this is not the case. I am loyal to the President. I have always been and will always be."

"And what will happen if more comes out in this blog thing, like the business at Harrods."

"Madam?"

"I'm sure you remember, a couple of months back, when Chafik was apprehended outside the store and charged with shoplifting. Of course, once it was explained that he and his family are so respected in their own country that shopkeepers would never accept payment from us for anything, and that Chafik had merely forgotten about the need to pay when abroad, once this had been explained, it was all sorted out. But if this, what do you call him, this blogger has got hold of it, then the truth will get distorted to further blacken his name."

Saali was faintly amused at the attempt to entrap him. He knew perfectly well that nothing of the sort had happened. He had been expecting something but nothing as crude or as obvious as this invention.

"Well, Madam, we shall just have to hope that it remains a secret, although, as things stand it seems to be very difficult to keep anything about Chafik a secret. Maybe we need to do something to counteract the bad publicity, something to build his reputation. It would help if he had a proper role, not in the Government, but maybe in the army. He is already nominally a general. We could have him assigned to a particular unit for a period of active service and, let's face it, a spell in the army here would keep him out of trouble abroad."

Saali knew that that was impossible. The army was powerful and would resist any attempt to have Chafik foisted on it.

"Now is not the time for Chafik to be playing at soldiers."

"There is the Air Squadron, Madam. Chafik has always wanted to learn to fly and he would have to have a junior officer rank. That would look good with the public, starting at the bottom."

The Air Squadron had been established by the President as a separate unit within the army structure, to counterbalance the power of the generals.

"We haven't got time for him to start at the bottom or anywhere else. This is getting us nowhere. I am going to ask you again, will you step down from the vice presidency or not?"

"I am sorry, Madam, but..."

"Then there is no point in continuing. This audience is finished."

With that the First lady clapped her hands and the same equerry appeared to escort Saali to his car.

THREE

THINGS WERE LOOKING up for Nasir. He was on the way back from one of his private lessons on the moped that Samira had given him a couple of weeks before. It was only a Honda 50cc but Nasir had never owned anything with wheels before, and he relished in the freedom and status it gave him. Even better, the university had reopened and, as well teaching his usual course, Nasir's hours had more than doubled, as he had been asked, if only for the time being, to cover for staff who had left to work abroad while the university was closed. Nasir still didn't have much money but what he had was more than ever before. All of which made him feel more and more uncertain about the blog. Certainly it was having its effects. So much anti-Regime graffiti was appearing on the streets that the authorities were hard pressed to keep on top of it, and within the university, the students and even the staff, were openly discussing the scandals surrounding Chafik and the corruption involving Basma. He'd even overheard conversations about it in the cafés he frequented, something unthinkable even just a few weeks before when people had been too scared to discuss anything political in public. This was both gratifying but increasingly worrying as well. Nasir knew that every member of the intelligence services would be being employed in discovering the identity of the author of the blog and he also knew that if the Vice President had managed to track him down, then sooner or later someone else was bound to do so too. Maybe it would be best to call it a day. He'd done his bit. Why continue to place himself in danger, especially now that life seemed to be getting better? Nasir had been wondering about his predicament for some time, without reaching a decision either way.

On his arrival home, Nasir walked the moped round to the back to lock it up in the small shed he had rented for the purpose. He spent the next hour with his son on his knee, reading to him from a storybook, pointing out the words and letters, getting him to repeat them, asking him questions to test his understanding. In that whole hour, Aliyah, his wife remained silent, preparing food and ignoring him. Nasir was only too aware that his marriage was a disaster and that his wife was cold and frigid towards him and he felt guilty about it. Saali had, of course been correct in saying that the marriage was arranged. Nasir had pleaded with his father against it when the matter had been broached and the pair introduced. In fact he had flatly refused but then his parents were killed in the crash on their way home from the capital after visiting him to try to make him change his mind and, out of some misguided feeling of loyalty towards them or maybe of guilt, he had done as they had wanted and gone through with the marriage. That was, however, as far as he had been prepared to go. They had expected him to leave the capital and return to the village to manage the land and the additional acres that came with the marriage. Indeed, those acres had been the reason for their choice of wife but Nasir had had no intention of leaving the capital or the university and had installed a tenant to run the farm and brought his bride to the small dwelling, in a run-down district of the capital which he had rented for them to live in. That the city was a completely alien environment to her, that she felt lonely and isolated, that she constantly pleaded with him for them to return to the village, of all that he was only too aware and it filled him with remorse, for he also knew that she too had pleaded with her parents that he was not the right choice for her. There had been a few occasions, when the university was shut and before he had established his translation contacts and private lessons, when he had thought of doing what was expected and returning to the countryside. She would have been happy, the marriage might have been saved but, somehow, Nasir could never face the return to his roots, to a way of life that he saw as backward and unchanging, regulated by outdated values, taboos and superstitions. The arrival of a son, Khalil, had reinforced his feelings. He wanted the boy to grow up amid the vibrancy of the city, to go to a proper school, then onto university, to travel and see the world, to be thoroughly modern.

Nasir's recollections of the next few minutes were only hazy. He vaguely remembered the sudden crashing noises, the door bursting open, the men charging in, the cries of the child, the screams of his wife. His son tossed aside, his wife sworn at, punched, ordered to be silent. He was dragged outside and tossed into the boot of a waiting car. In total darkness, as the car sped away, Nasir struggled to regain some sort of composure, to stop shaking. It was some minutes before he was able to think coherently. Undoubtedly it was the security forces, probably he was on his way to No 42, and almost certainly he had been linked to the blog and that could only mean torture to extract the names of others and then, if Saali was correct, execution. Nasir remembered the previous occasion, the lashes, the pain. It was going to be a lot worse this time and he doubted whether he would have the inner strength to resist their demands, even though the lives of others depended on it.

When the car stopped and the boot was opened, Nasir could tell it wasn't No 42. He was marched at gunpoint into a nondescript modern building and bundled into a lift that descended down into some lower basement and was then thrown into a cell. It was at least a couple of hours before anything happened and those hours were deliberately intended as part of the torture or at least as a form of torment for where one is made to wait for the unknown but knowing that it is going to be excruciating, one's mind goes into imagination overdrive.

At last Nasir, simply terrified by then, was escorted, again at gunpoint, into a room furnished only with a long table, from which hung down shackles for wrists and feet. The guards made him strip, blindfolded him, manacled him, front down, onto the table and then left the room. There he was left for at least another hour until his torturer arrived. Nasir never saw this man but he would remember his voice for as long as he lived.

"Good afternoon, Mr Raziq. I would like you to give me some information. If you do and the information is true we will cease this business immediately and you will be free to go. I should warn you that you will give us this information eventually whether you want to or not, so you might as well do it straight away and save yourself a lot of pain.

Now before I start, let me ask you a question. Do you know what a sadist is, Mr Raziq? I am sure you do but allow me to remind you anyway. A sadist is a person who enjoys inflicting pain on others. Now can you guess what I am, Mr Raziq? I am a sadist, Mr Raziq. My job is inflicting pain and I love my job, in fact it isn't so much a job to me, as more of a calling, a vocation. Now, I am not the sort of sadist who goes in at the deep end. I like to start small, so to speak, and work my way up to the more, how shall I put it, the more heavy stuff. So listen to this, Mr Raziq, it is the sound of the cane I am going to hit you with. Just a cane, you think, like a schoolteacher on a child. This isn't going to be as bad as I thought, you are thinking. Well, Mr Raziq, remember it is only the beginning. Tomorrow will bring something far worse and so it will go on, day after day. And be aware, Mr Raziq, that although it is only a cane, it is a very slender cane, supple but strong. It will impart exquisite pain. And you should know that I am also an artist, Mr Raziq, and I am going to use this cane to draw a beautiful geometric design on your back and buttocks. A beautiful design of the sort you can find in any of our great mosques and public buildings. I think it will take about half an hour and a hundred or so strokes. A hundred strokes of pain. Now, before I begin, is there anything you would like to tell me?"

The cane had made a whooshing noise at it cut through the air. Nasir could only anticipate the pain it would cause. The only thing to do was to deny everything in the hope that this was just a warning, as his detention in No 42 had been.

"Tell you? What can I tell you? What do you want me to tell you? I know nothing. I mind my own business and keep out of trouble. You've got the wrong person; I haven't got anything to tell."

"Come now, Mr Raziq. We both know that there is a concerted effort going on to undermine the presidency and you work in the university which is a hot bed of dissidence, so don't tell me that you know nothing. We monitor the university and it has come to our attention that you have conversations in English outside the classroom. Now, why would you have conversations in English unless you didn't want anyone listening to know what you are talking about; unless, perhaps, you were planning a new act of dissent?"

For a moment Nasir thought he had misheard. Surely he wasn't there simply because he had been speaking in a foreign language, in English.

"Are you serious? I teach English at the university. Do you mean that you have got me here for doing my job?"

"I am very serious, Mr Raziq. Your job is to teach English in the classroom. Why would you be having discussions in English in the cafeteria?"

"But it is only a way of practising it with my students. This is crazy."

Nasir's mind was racing. If they had got him down there for some idiotic reason then it only went to show how desperate they were but if that was all they had detained him for then it also meant that they hadn't connected him to the blog.

"Well, Mr Raziq, being told that what I do is crazy does make me feel rather angry. I think we should begin."

With that Nasir felt a searing pain as the cane made its first contact with his skin. His torturer worked methodically, firstly with horizontal strokes across back and buttocks and then intersecting these with vertical strokes. The worst pain came later when diagonal strokes cut into the wheals made by the earlier ones. Nasir screamed with each stroke and felt that he was drowning in a sea of pain. It seemed to last an eternity and not once was there a pause to ask whether he was ready to talk. In the end the torturer spoke in admiration of the pattern he had created but expressed concern that the blood was rather disfiguring his fine work.

"Tomorrow I shall make a start on your front. It will be rather more brutal; broken ribs can be very painful and cause lasting damage if not properly mended. After that I have pliers that are very good at pulling out fingernails and toenails. One of my specialities is sewing eyelids open. Have you ever tried to sleep with your eyes open? Not being able to blink will mean that your eyes will dry up. The pain is terrible. In the end you will go permanently blind and all that before we have made a start on the more delicate parts of your anatomy with the use of electricity. Ponder my words, Mr Raziq. I will see you in the morning."

That night was the worst that Nasir had ever had to endure. His back felt as if it was on fire, even the smallest movement was excruciating and there was no relief from the pain all night long. What made it even worse was that his cell was hot and airless. There was no cool draught to ease the burning. Sleep was impossible, all he could do was to try to lie as still as possible, waiting for the morning and whatever it might bring. As he lay there he tried to bring soothing thoughts to mind; the face of his son, memories of his parents, the days of his graduation from high school and university. It gave a little relief but not much. He also considered the situation and whether there was anything he could do to alleviate it. There was nothing he could say to his torturer about the university, no names he could or would give. He could only reiterate that the conversations were a form of practise for his students, which anyone could have heard and that any of those within hearing might have been able to speak English and understand what was said. There had been nothing suspicious about them. Towards the dawn another thought came to mind and a plan began to form in Nasir's mind. It was a long shot but it was a possibility and it was the only thing he could think of.

Nasir had no idea of the time when they came for him. They took him to the same room, blindfolded and tied him to the same table, this time facing upwards so that the pain of his wounds flared into a new intensity as his back came into contact with the hard surface. Once again he was left for an hour or so to contemplate his fate and then he heard the door open and the footsteps of his torturer and tormentor as he entered the room.

"Well, Mr Raziq, I take it you slept well and are looking forward to the day ahead. Before we make a start I wonder if there is anything you would like to tell me now, so that we can bring this unfortunate ordeal to an end."

"There is one thing I would like to say," answered Nasir, his voice hoarse and faltering.

"And what would that be, Mr Raziq?"

"Only that the Vice President of the Republic is going to be pretty angry when he hears about this. I give English lessons to one of his relatives and Mr al-Malimi personally interviewed me for the post. It goes without saying that he must have had me checked out by his security people and found me suitable, so it makes a nonsense of my being here simply because someone heard me speaking English in a cafeteria. In fact a lesson is scheduled for this afternoon. They'll want to know why I'm not there. You'll have some explaining to do."

There was no reply. Nasir simply heard the door open and close as the torturer left the room. Some minutes later the door opened again and a different voice asked for the details of the person to whom he was to give the lesson. Nasir gave the names of the girl and of her parents and their address in the Special Zone. After that he was left alone again. Time passed, maybe an hour or so and then the door opened again. His blindfold was undone and his shackles removed. He was told to get dressed. A few minutes later guards led him, gently this time, out of the building and into a waiting car that took him back to his home.

FOUR

NOT HAVING KEYS, Nasir knocked on the door. After several seconds when nothing happened, he pressed gently against it and found that it swung open at a crazy angle, the result of the forced entry by the security people the previous day. Inside it was empty; there was no sign of Aliyah or Khalil. He called out for them, saying it was only him, thinking they might be hiding in fear in some corner. He looked in each room but they were not there. Only a bit later did he discover that the big suitcase was missing, along with various item of clothing. They had gone and Nasir could only surmise it was back to the village and to her father. Next, he checked that the tablet computer was still in its hiding place; it was. In fact, everything was in its place, nothing else was missing. The security forces had simply come for him. If they had also searched the apartment it would have been ransacked but even his mobile phone was there, still plugged into its charger and the wall socket.

Nasir, his back still throbbing with pain, struggled to think of what he should do. Maybe he could take himself to the public hospital or call up a doctor but such things cost money and he had little left until his next pay packet. He opened the fridge and found it almost empty of food but there was the big water bottle that they always kept full and Nasir, not having eaten or drunk for almost twenty four hours, gulped down most of its contents and then poured the rest over his face and onto his back. It brought relief but not for long. The realisation came that if he couldn't afford medical help, he would have to tend to his wounds himself to prevent the possibility of infection. At the very least he needed to cleanse his back of its dried blood but when he tried to take off his shirt he found that it was stuck and he was afraid that trying to pull it off would take whatever skin was left with it. Beginning to feel desperate he checked his list of phone contacts for anyone he could turn to for help and while doing this he remembered Samira. He'd put the slip of paper containing her number under the hidden tablet computer and retrieving it, he dialled and waited. She answered, he explained what had happened and she said she would be there within an hour.

Along the way Samira stopped at a pharmacy and she arrived with bandages, cotton wool, ointments and creams. She smiled to see him but grimaced when he turned round to show her his back. Blood was oozing through the fabric of his shirt and when she tried to remove it he screamed in pain.

"Maybe if you stand in the shower the water will loosen the shirt. You have got a shower, haven't you?"

Nasir nodded.

"You'll have to take your trousers off. I expect your pants are stuck too. Don't worry, I'm very broad minded."

The shower gave out little more than a trickle of water. It was cold too but the feel of it on his back brought instant relief from the pain. Once his clothes were thoroughly wet, she took hold of them gently and pulled them away from his skin, first the shirt and then his pants. Standing naked in the shower, even with his back to her, Nasir felt embarrassed but she said nothing and taking and wetting balls of cotton wool, she began to dab gently at the bloody mess of his back and buttocks. After a few minutes she noticed that he was shivering in the cold water and led him, wet and naked, into the bedroom where she had him lie down while she continued the delicate work of cleansing. Finally, she gently rubbed antiseptic ointment all over his back and buttocks. At any other time such a motion would have been arousing but lying there, with the pain returned, he just wanted it to be over as soon as possible.

"There,' she said at last, 'that's the best I can do. Really you should see a doctor. I think it is better not to try to use bandages, just to leave your skin open to the air. I'm going to go out now and buy you a few things. Maybe I should get you a mosquito net too. I won't be long."

Nasir must have dozed off while Samira was away for the next thing he knew she was standing over him, holding a bowl of hot soup, together with some fresh bread. She put them down on the bedside table.

"You'll have to sit up to eat. Here,' she said, smiling and handing him a towel, 'you can use this to cover yourself."

While he was eating she asked him about his ordeal. She was very insistent that he told her everything about the reason for his arrest, what he had told the torturer and why he had been released. He gave as much detail as he could remember.

"Was it ok to mention the Vice President and the lessons? It was the only thing I could think of that might get them to stop."

"In this case, I think so,' she answered. 'If they weren't connecting you to the blog I don't think it will have done any damage. I was out when the call came through. Hatti took it. She told me that someone had asked if you gave Yasmin English lessons and wondered whether she had done right to say yes. I feared something was up and called you straightaway but there was no answer. I tried calling Saali too to see if he knew anything but he was in some meeting and couldn't be disturbed. I was even thinking of coming here but wondered what your wife would make of it. Have you spoken to her yet? Has she gone to her parents? It must have been very frightening for her."

"No, not yet. The...the situation with my wife, between us I mean, is difficult. To tell you the truth, I'm more concerned about my son. It must have been terrifying for him. I hope it doesn't do any lasting psychological damage. Yes, I think she has gone to her father's."

Nasir didn't say so but the thought had already struck him that Aliyah might not be willing to return, might never return and that would mean that he would be rid of her at last.

"You should at least call to let them know that you're ok. No, I know that you're not ok but you know what I mean. You are home, you are alive and you are hurt but you will recover. Now, Yasmin will be back from school in a bit so I have to go. I'll just arrange the net first. We don't want any mossies dining on your back tonight."

Samira busied herself with the mosquito net, while Nasir sat watching. When she had finished, she gathered up her things and told him she would be back in the morning. As she took her leave she bent low and kissed him lightly on the forehead.

"I'm so pleased that you got out of there."

Under the mosquito net and with the ceiling fan turning slowly to blow a gentle breeze on his back, Nasir slept for several hours after Samira had left. When he awoke the daylight was fading and he was hungry. In the fridge he found pitta, hummus and goats cheese. As he ate his thoughts turned to his wife and son and to the conversation he needed to make. It would not be easy. Aliyah did not have her own phone, so he would have to call her father and her father had already made his feelings towards him perfectly clear. Even so, Nasir was not prepared for the torrent of abuse that came his way. As soon as her father answered and was aware that it was

Nasir calling, he launched into a tirade against him, how he was a good for nothing, how he had made his daughter's life hell, how he was not fit to be a father, how he had ignored his responsibilities to them, to her family, the land and the village. How he brought shame and dishonour on them all by being arrested. There were no questions about what had happened to him after he had been carted off, not the slightest concern for what he might have suffered and when Nasir asked to speak to his wife, the line simply went dead.

Samira came the next day and for several days after. She came with an antiseptic spray that her doctor had prescribed that was easier on his back and buttocks than the cream. She always came in wearing a scarf that she took off immediately, shaking her hair back into shape. Once or twice she was in casual slacks but usually she wore a skirt that ended at least a couple of inches above the knee. Above that she wore loose fitting blouses but which were sometimes sufficiently transparent to show what she was wearing underneath. Each day she stayed for an hour or so, bringing fresh food, bottled water and soft drinks. She tended his wounds, prepared food and talked about Saali or places she had been, places so far away Nasir scarcely knew where they were on the map. Each time she went away, Nasir spent ages thinking about her, about her beauty, her self-confidence, her calmness, her modernity and about that kiss. Very soon he was completely fixated on her and thought about little else. She was everything that he wanted in a woman, everything that he had dreamed of when he had broken away from the village and embraced the modern world and she was also everything that his wife would never be. Yet, when he asked her about herself, her past, her upbringing, her parents, she brushed the questions aside, so that, after nearly a week of her visits, he knew little more about her than he had done before. She was educated, that was obvious, and well travelled. She was a nanny too, although that didn't seem to fit well. But she was also the Vice President's go-between, his confident; where did that come from and what did it mean? This aura of mystique only increased his fascination with her.

For several days he could hardly move, because movement cause such pain in his back and buttocks. She sprayed the antiseptic and dabbed at his back with cotton wool, urging him to stay calm, saying that he was getting better. And gradually, scabs formed, the pain decreased and he was able to tolerate a shirt again. Finally, when she said he was recovered and did not need her any more, he felt a sense of panic that she would leave his world. In that moment his desire for her took control and he reached out to embrace her. The reaction came as brutally as if she had slapped his face.

"No, don't, please stop. You are married, you shouldn't be thinking about me this way. You have responsibilities. Think of your wife and son, they are the ones you should be thinking about, not me. I am here because you needed me to nurse you and because Saali needs you to be well. That is all. I'm sorry, I have to go now."

FIVE

THE SUDDEN TURBULENCE jolted Saali awake. Instinctively he felt for the seat belt to make sure it was fastened. That done, he gripped the armrests as the plane shuddered about. Actually, Saali quite liked a bit of turbulence, as long as it wasn't too violent; it reminded him of his early flying days when he had piloted a two-seater Tomahawk that used to get blown about in the airstreams.

Saali was on his way to New York for the opening session of the annual General Assembly of the United Nations. It was a visit he usually looked forward to. New York, in late September, still retained some of its summer warmth, so the temperature there was just perfect after the sweltering North African heat. Saali also enjoyed the vibrancy of the city, of just being able to wander Manhattan streets unrecognised and maybe to take in a Broadway theatre if anything decent was playing. Last time he'd been to a new production of Arthur Miller's,

Death of a Salesman, a play he had first seen many years before in London and found it to be even more moving than previously, although maybe that was because he was, by then, at an age where he could more easily identify with Willy Loman's personal sense of failure. Above all, Saali enjoyed his visits to New York because he got to stay with his old friend, Ahmed Saqqaf, in the Consulate. Ahmed was, in reality, the country's top diplomat in the country following the breakdown in diplomatic relations that led to the recall of the U.S. ambassador, followed by a tit for tat action and their replacements by chargé d'affaires. This breakdown reflected the growing isolation of the country that accompanied the decline in its international standing, this being a result of the ever increasing criticism of its appalling human rights record. This record was no worse than that of several other Middle Eastern countries but they had sufficient oil reserves or were of such strategic importance that their violations were generally ignored. This isolation did have one benefit though; there were fewer invitations to Saali to attend evening social functions, something he didn't mind at all.

In fact, Saali had asked the President to send the Deputy Foreign Minister to this year's session instead of himself. The President, knowing how much Saali looked forward to it and thinking the request was out of concern for his own health, had refused and insisted that Saali attend. Saali was worried that his absence, even for just a week or so, might undermine his position in the country. The First Lady's access to the President would allow her to press the case for his replacement by Chafik and to generally plot against him. There was also the possibility that the President might die while he was away and they might use his absence to appoint Chafik or one of Basma's brothers as interim president. Saali had made plans to use the President's funeral as the opportunity for a speech to the nation that would strengthen his position; that would be impossible if the funeral took place while he was in New York.

Saali had another concern. Mr Raziq had used his name in order to get himself released from detention. Saali could understand why but nevertheless, his name and Nasir's were now linked. He could just picture the situation if Basma were to be told about it, how she might distort it to sow seeds of doubt in the President's mind.

"Did you know, my dear husband, that Saali is connected, no more than that, he is a good friend of a known dissident and trouble maker and Saali actually got this dissident released after he was detained for questioning about terrorist offences? Not that I have anything other than the utmost respect for the Vice President but this does throw a new light on things..."

Ahmed met Saali in person at JFK. The two old friends embraced warmly, exchanging pleasantries about the flight, their health and one or two mutual acquaintances. Both were rather shocked at how frail the other looked but neither said anything. The journey to the Consulate took ages; the traffic was awful. On the way they continued to reminisce about old times. They had first met many years before as students at the

Sorbonne. Ahmed had gone on to do research and become a lecturer, working in a succession of universities in several countries, until he achieved his ambition of a Chair in Linguistics back in France. Despite his lack of diplomatic experience, when the position of Consular General had come available at the same time as Ahmed had left his university job amid a scandal over his relationships with female undergraduates, Saali had appointed him to the New York post, knowing it would give him the opportunity to meet up with his old mate at least once a year.

Later, after Saali had slept off the worst effects of the journey, they dined together with Ahmed's wife and her sister, who was also visiting. It was only after coffee, when the women had left them to their brandies that the two men were able to talk properly about the situation back home. That Ahmed was aware of the President's cancer came as no surprise. While the general public were still in the dark, it was difficult to keep that sort of thing from those in important positions and rumours had been flying around. Nor was Saali surprised at Ahmed's interest in the blog; after all it was freely available everywhere on the internet and there was a small but influential group of disaffected nationals in the U.S. who would have been following it and publicising it as widely as possible. Saali, however, was taken aback when Ahmed told him outright that some people were linking him to it.

"There is a lot of speculation that you might be behind it; after all, how many other people would be privy to all that information? People are also wondering if you have designs on the presidency yourself. I don't expect you to admit anything, I just want you to be aware that this is what others are saying and this makes your situation precarious, dangerous even. Everyone knows that Chafik is intended to be the next president. You need to be very careful."

Later, at various intervals during the following week, basically the same message was relayed to Saali by a number of foreign diplomats. Saali doubted that they were genuinely concerned for his welfare, more likely just prodding for information to relay back to their governments. He remained stony faced throughout, saying nothing.

On his last day in New York Ahmed called him up on his mobile phone to ask if he'd heard the news from back home. Saali's immediate thought was that the president had died but no, there had been a terrorist attack in the capital and several people had been killed. The terrorists, three of them, had been pursued and then holed up in a disused warehouse on the outskirts. Chafik had personally led an attack on the building with members of the security forces and had later emerged, brandishing his revolver and with the three dead terrorists being dragged out. The attack on the warehouse had been shown live on the two state television channels, which had also shown later scenes of a jubilant Chafik waving at cheering crowds from a balcony of the National Palace.

Later that day Saali telephoned the recently

appointed Minister of the Interior and congratulated him on his handling of the incident.

"By the way, where did you get hold of the three victims, the ones who were supposed to be the terrorists?"

"Oh, just ordinary prisoners. I had three people selected who were already condemned to death so they were going to die soon anyway."

Later that day Saali caught his plane home. The journey meant changing flights at Paris Charles de Gaulle. Usually he would have stopped off for a day or two in Paris to see an old friend (there were rumours that Saali had a secret lover in Paris) but this time he caught the first available plane. He needed to get back in case anything happened.

SIX

THE MINIBUS WAS HOT, crowded and very noisy, with
the radio blasting out music at full volume. Nasir was
jammed in and uncomfortable. It didn't help that this was
the same stretch of road on which his parents had died in
the head on collision that left five others dead as well. His
mind kept going back to the trauma he had felt on
learning the news and in its aftermath. Once past the
spot, however, Nasir became calmer and his mind
reflected on the events of the past two days. Having rung
beforehand to announce his visit, Nasir had known that
his father in law was always going to be difficult but he
had not anticipated the level of animosity or that his wife
and son would have been packed off somewhere and that
he would not be allowed to see them. In the end he had
lost his temper, swore at the man and shouted, in a fit of
rage, that if that was the case and he could not even talk
to his wife or son, he might as well not be married at all
and would divorce her on the spot. That brought the old

fool to his senses because even he knew that a divorced woman was regarded as 'used goods' and would just become a burden on him. Either that or she would have to be married off to some old man and live a life of drudgery. Nasir had gone on to insist, much to the other's displeasure that he would meet his wife and son alone and that they would talk things through without interference from him.

It turned out that Aliyah and Khalil were only a few minutes away at a neighbour's house and her father, leaving Khalil there, brought Aliyah across and then left the two of them alone. To begin with neither found it easy to speak but then she asked about his treatment in the jail and broke into tears when he pulled up his shirt to show her his back. Somehow he hadn't anticipated such a response.

"Do you want to know why, why they did this to me? All because someone heard me speaking in English to some of my students outside the classroom and reported me for supposedly plotting some act of rebellion, when all we were discussing was football or the movies or some such thing. This is the sort of country we are living in. But I'm sorry that you had such a shock. One of them punched you, didn't he? Was it bad, were you bruised. What about Khalil? How did he take it? Is he all right now?"

Aliyah told him that the punch had just winded her, that was all. Khalil had screamed at the time and cried a lot afterwards. He will be overjoyed to see his father again. Still tearful, she asked for his forgiveness for having left the house in the city when her duty was to have stayed and waited for him. When Nasir said it was the sensible thing to have done, she smiled and, for the first time in many months, she hugged him. At the same time, she undid her scarf to let her long brown hair fall freely.

It almost seemed to Nasir, as she held him, that the marriage might be saved but then there was the future to discuss. The proper thing to do would be to take them both back to the capital but he knew that this would only bring about a continuation of their previous unhappiness. Aliyah had hated it there and she would always hate it. Neither though, could he ever consent to live with them there, in that remote and backward place, cut off from all things modern. And uppermost in his mind was the boy and his future and how that could be assured the way he wanted if he was to be left there in such a backwater, for the social rules, enforceable in law, were that the children must stay with their mother in the case of marital breakdown.

The impasse was broken by the arrival of Khalil who had learned of his father's arrival and rushed over to meet him. After the initial greetings and the unwrapping of presents that Nasir had brought with him, the boy wanted Nasir to meet his new best friend and so the three of them walked out into the village, husband and wife each holding a hand and swinging Khalil between them. Later Nasir went across to inspect the family home and fields. His wife had warned him that the tenant was lazy, had let the place go and the fields become infested with weeds but Nasir was shocked at just how dilapidated his old home looked. It did not help matters that the tenant was asleep on the front porch when he arrived, even though the heat of the day had already passed and all the other younger men of the village were out in the fields. After a brief tour of the house and the land Nasir had expressed his displeasure and said he would have to consider the situation.

Actually it was the situation that provided a solution to the marital dilemma. Nasir proposed to Aliyah that he should dismiss the tenant and that she would take over the house and fields. Whenever the need arose, at harvest time for instance, she could employ extra labour. He would visit once a month or even more often, something that was all too common in a village where few employment possibilities were evident and where several of the married men had to work away from home. In this way they would give the impression of being just another married couple, even though the situation between them was difficult. She would not have to live in a place she hated and he would be able to see the boy regularly. Nasir had one proviso when he suggested the arrangement to his wife; Khalil must live with him and go to school in the capital once he was passed the primary stage. Aliyah agreed and seemed more than happy with a solution that allowed her to keep her social standing as a married woman. Whether they would share a bed on his visits was something left unsaid and that night he slept on a sofa.

About twenty kilometres from the capital Nasir's

phone buzzed. In all that noise it was difficult to hear what Samira was saying but it was clear that something was up. In the end he had to ask her to shout. She asked where he was and then told him he must get off at the stop before last and wait for her there. She would explain then. Nasir did as he was instructed, getting off at a place on the dusty outskirts of the city, his mind racing with all the various possibilities of what might have happened and all of them involving danger. By the time he spotted her car, about thirty minutes later, he was really worked up and agitated.

Samira greeted him with a smile but no words. She drove off but then turned into a side street and parked.

"I'm sorry Nasir, it's really quite serious. The lady who takes the stuff to Malta has been arrested. Saali is worried that she will talk and that she will give them your name. She might already have done so. We can't be sure. Saali says you mustn't go to your home. They might be waiting for you. You need to go into hiding."

Nasir didn't know what to say. An hour before it had looked as though he had settled on some kind of future, now he was basically a hunted man.

"Where should I go? Where can I hide? Should I go back to my wife in the village?"

"You can come with me. Saaali says I should hide you. My place will be safe. They will be sure to check out your wife, pay her a visit. You should warn her but not give anything away, of course. I'm sorry about this Nasir. Saali has someone in No 42. He is keeping him informed. They know it is about the blog. Somehow they have connected her to it. That's all I know at the moment. Saali will speak to me again this evening. He wants to know if there is anything at your place that would be incriminating."

"A small laptop, I use to write the blog. I wipe the information on it regularly but I don't know, maybe they could still get at the files. Nothing else, I think."

"Where is it exactly? Saali will send someone to pick it up."

Nasir explained about the hiding place and Samira started to write a text message with the details. A new thought entered Nasir's mind, that maybe all this was a trick. That he had served his usefulness and was now being got rid of. They would get rid of the laptop and then get rid of him. He tried to push the thought away; she had always been kind to him, she had nursed him back to health. He had to believe that she was not deceiving him. He had to trust her. What else could he do?

Samira's apartment was in a modern block in a complex, near the city's business centre. When they were about a mile away she turned into a side road and told Nasir that the complex was gated, with cameras that filmed everything going in and out. They should not be seen together. He would have to lie on the back seat and be covered with a rug. Furthermore he had to stay like that once she had gone, for at least half an hour until it was fully dark. Only then would it be safe for him to leave the car. She gave him a key to the building, told him to take the lift to the eighth floor and gave him the number of her apartment.

In the back, alone and covered with the rug, Nasir gradually calmed down. His thoughts focussed on Samira. Once again he realised he knew next to nothing about her. She had some sort of job in the Special Zone but that couldn't pay much, so who was she, where did she come from, how did she live? What was she to Saali? Was she his mistress or maybe his daughter? And how ironic that he was going to stay in her place when she had already rejected his advances. Then he began to panic that he would forget the number of her apartment and not be able to find her. He steadied himself by putting the number into his phone and trying to concentrate on something else, something nice, like his son and the things they had done together.

Eventually, when he had checked and was satisfied that the light had gone, Nasir pulled away the rug and peered out of the window. The car was parked among others and the entrance to the building, lit by a single light, was about twenty yards away. Just as he was about to make a move he saw the door to the building open and a couple emerged and came in his direction. Nasir quickly pulled the rug back over him and waited. A couple of minutes passed before he heard an engine start up and the sound of a car pulling away. He waited a few minutes more and then checked, opened the car door and slipped out, crouching low as he made his way through the parked cars, key in hand and ready. Once inside the building, the lift was directly in front of him. A new feeing of panic gripped him when he saw the light indicating that it was descending and that it was probably occupied. It was coming down too fast for him to get away, so he stood still and turned aside to look at a notice board, so that he would not be facing anyone who came out. When the doors opened he heard people talking animatedly and continued to look aside as they walked past him.

Samira welcomed him with a smile and ushered him inside. The door opened onto a small hall, with doors off, which led to a large lounge, expensively furnished.

"There's only one bedroom, I'm afraid but I've got a beach lounger or you could use the sofa. Here, let me show you around."

Samira showed him the rest of the apartment. It reminded Nasir of the places in the Special Zone. He could only dream of such affluence for himself.

"There is a lovely view of the city but I think it is better not to open the curtains at night. You can see in the morning. Now, please make yourself comfortable while I get us something to eat. Are you ok with everything, not a vegetarian or any allergies or anything like that? You could put the TV on or there is a music player. Whatever you want."

Samira disappeared into the kitchen but returned a few minutes later holding a bottle of white wine and two glasses.

"It's quite dry, is that alright?"

Nasir paused before answering.

"I do... no, yes, that's fine."

The wine went straight to his head. His last alcohol had been as a fifteen year old. He'd gone home drunk and his father had thrashed him. At least it helped to make him a little more relaxed. During the meal Samira asked him about his wife and the weekend and Nasir found himself telling her everything, even that he would have rather divorced her had it not been for Khalil.

"So basically it's an arrangement to save face. Whenever I'm there we'll put up the pretence of being a married couple and that way she'll keep her social standing in the village but basically the marriage is finished. I should never have gone through with it in the first place. It's not her fault, we just aren't suited. It's just for appearances sake. When he reaches secondary age and comes to live with me, I expect I'll see less and less of her."

"You really love your son."

"I have such hopes for him. I want him to get a proper education, go to university, get a job in one of the professions, travel the world. God knows if I'll be able to help make any of that happen now I'm mixed up in this mess. I'm beginning to rue the day I ever started the blog and met Saali."

"And me?"

Nasir paused, embarrassed.

"No, not you. I think of you often."

There was a long pause and then Samira started to clear away. Nasir offered to wash up but she would have none of it and turned on the TV instead. An American soap was starting soon and she didn't want to miss it. The television helped. He didn't have to talk, to make polite conversation.

Sometime later the phone rang. It was Saali. Samira talked to him for a minute or so than handed the receiver to Nasir.

"He wants to talk to you."

The news was bad. She had talked and given his name. He was to stay put, not put a foot outside. The authorities did not know about Samira's place. She was not on their antennae. He would be safe there. He had the laptop. Try not to worry. He'd arrange something. Tomorrow would bring a change. He couldn't say more.

"I'm sorry," said Samira when the call had finished.

"It's not your fault. I don't know what I've have done without you. At least I'm safe here."

"I'll get you some sheets. If you turn off the air con you won't need blankets. Is that alright?"

"Of course, whatever you think."

"I could get you a whisky or a brandy. It might help."

"Lord no. The wine has had enough effect already. I'm not really used to drinking."

"I know. I remember you had orange juice that first time in the Special Zone but I thought the wine would help break the ice. It's quite a difficult situation, isn't it?"

Nasir smiled.

"Thank you. The wine worked."

Samira brought out the lounger and sheets and she found a spare toothbrush for him. Once he had finished in the bathroom and was arranging the bedding, Samira's bedroom door opened and she stood in the doorway in a short dressing gown.

"It would be more comfortable in here."

Nasir wondered if he had misunderstood.

"I thought... I mean... you said... before...in my place..."

Samira undid the dressing gown to let it fall open.

"I changed my mind. You said your marriage is over. Are you coming?

SEVEN

SA'ALI AL-MALIMI WAS in low spirits as Raafi drove him to the presidential palace. Things were not turning out as he had planned and he had an onerous task to perform. In fact, things were getting very difficult indeed now that they had broadcast Raziq's name and face all over the airwaves and were combing the streets for him. That coupled with the fact that the President was still hanging on months after he should have been dead. Another problem was that the continued milking for all it was worth of Chafik's supposed act of bravery against the terrorists, seemed to be paying off in terms of the public approval of him. All in all it had to be accepted that it was time to act. Leaving it even a few more days might prove disastrous, especially as Raziq's name was sure to be linked to his own. Even so, it would be a difficult thing to do after all these years of friendship, perhaps the most difficult thing he had ever done.

Saali found the President looking decidedly unwell.

He found it difficult to manage the few paces into the garden, even using a walking frame. It made Saali think that the end was near anyway, so why not wait for nature to take its course. Maybe, however, the thought that death was near anyway would make it easier.

"I think this may be it," Baashir said wearily and in a faltering voice to Saali. "To tell you the truth, I'm tired of trying to fight it."

"Nonsense," said Saali, "you look fine. You've got months left."

"Perhaps but then again. One thing though," said Baashir, "I'd like you to be there when it happens. My oldest and dearest friend, it would be a comfort to me. Will you do that for me? I've instructed Basma that that's what I want."

"Of course, of course but we should be positive and hope for the future."

Baashir's request pleased Saali. It meant that he didn't have to come up with an excuse for hanging around.

"Tell you what. Have a sherbet lemon. You know how you like them. In fact I think they may be a factor in your longevity."

The President smiled and nodded and Saali reached into his pocket but did not take a sweet out of the packet. Instead he paused for a few seconds, pondering, before taking one of the two that were in a separate bag. He unwrapped it and handed it to Baashir, who crunched it as he always did and then asked for another which he sucked for some minutes before speaking again.

"Do you know they've uncovered who might be behind the blog? It's good news. The new Minister of the Interior might prove to be better than the other idiots I've had to put up with. He told me that you phoned him about the terrorist incident. Clever of you to have guessed that it was a set up. How did you know?"

"Oh, just a guess, as you said. It's had the desired effect?"

"Chafik has never been so popular. It was all Basma's idea."

"I guessed that as well."

"Oh dear, but then again you were always the clever one. Let's hope the public are more gullible and remain convinced. You know, I'm beginning to have high hopes for Chafik. I know he's been a tearaway but then we all had our days, well I certainly did, but I honestly think that he's matured a lot recently. We had a long chat the other day and he talked about all the things he wanted to do as president. How he wanted to continue my work of modernisation and democratisation. I think the Republic will be safe in his hands."

"Well, let's hope so. He's certainly raised a few eyebrows in the past. Perhaps the presidency will be the making of him."

Saali knew full well that what he and the President had just said was make believe but it was as well to reassure Baashir that he accepted that Chafik would become president, even though that was the last thing he intended.

After only a few minutes in the garden the President

complained of tiredness and asked to be taken indoors. Saali helped him inside and to his bedroom and then took his leave. He had another appointment to keep; Basma had summoned him to see her. This time she didn't keep him waiting or make him sit through the formality of tea and sweetmeats; she got straight to the point.

"He's a lot worse, isn't he? It really is time now to relinquish the vice presidency to Chafik. The succession must go through seamlessly."

She was surprised at his answer.

"Yes, I agree, Madam. He does look a lot worse today. It's sad to see. I think it should all be done as openly as possible so there is no question about it. I suggest that we do it tomorrow, maybe in the Senate if Baashir can manage it but here if not. In front of the TV cameras. Get the Leader of the House, a few other dignitaries as well and make it a formal handover. I resign and Baashir appoints Chafik. It would be like a coronation. What do you think?"

Basma beamed with pleasure.

"I hadn't considered doing it like that, I'd just thought about making a formal announcement but, no, that's a brilliant idea. There will be no doubt. Can you arrange it? I'll make sure that Baashir is ready."

"Of course, Madam. Leave it to me. I'll phone through with the details when it is all prepared. There is one other thing, Madam," Saali paused. "He's asked me to be with him when the time comes. I don't want to impose myself on the family at such a difficult time but he's asked."

"No, I mean yes, he's already talked to me about it. Of course. You're like family anyway, a dear friend to all of us. Of course you must be present. Now, let's have some tea. "

Basma clapped her hands and a servant entered with a trolley of savouries and cakes. The tea arrived a few minutes later and Basma, for the first time that Saali could remember, insisted on pouring. He'd never her seen her smile so genuinely.

Even before the first cup was finished a servant knocked and urgently asked to enter. The President had taken a turn for the worse and was asking for them. They hurried to Baashir's bedroom. He was lying, eyes closed, his breathing laboured. He roused a little when Basma took his arm but was unable to speak.

"Get Chafik here and the doctor. Get them here immediately."

It took Baashir four hours to die. During that time Saali remained in the background as much as possible and did not speak, even though he felt profound sorrow at the passing of a friendship that went back to his childhood. He felt sorrow but no guilt for what he had done. Baashir was dying anyway. The important thing was that Chafik could not automatically step into his father's footsteps. The rest was already planned.

The President's personal physician recorded the time of death. Basma was stony faced, Chafik crying.

"There should be a post mortem. His ending was rather rapid, faster than I would have expected."

Saali reacted before Basma could respond.

"Cut him up, are you serious? He's been dying of cancer for months. What good will cutting him up do? Just sign the death certificate and let's be done with it."

Basma said nothing but Chafik, choking on the words, agreed with Saali. He did not want his father to be cut up and dissected. The cause of death was clear enough. As he and his mother were bent over the body of his father and their attention diverted, Saali took out his phone and sent two messages that he had already composed and saved as drafts.

Saali got up and walked to the door.

"Where are you going?" demanded Basma.

"Just to the bathroom. A call of nature. It's been a long time."

"But come straight back. There are things to discuss. The situation has changed."

Basma was deadly serious. Saali knew that she was focussed on the succession.

"Of course, Madam. A few minutes."

Saali left the room but found himself accompanied by an official.

"What are you doing?"

"Madam instructed me to come with you."

"Come with me? Well, I'm telling you that I know where the toilet is and I've been managing to use it all these years all by myself and I don't need any help from you. Go away."

"But she insisted."

"Well, I'm insisting too. I'll tell you what, you wait here and when I'm finished we can go back together."

"I don't…"

"It's not a request. It is an order. I am the Vice President of the Republic and I'm not having anyone come with me when I go to the toilet. That's final. Wait here."

It worked and Saali went on alone. There was a toilet next to the President's bedroom but Basma did not allow anyone, other than family to use it. The staff toilets, in the direction of which Saali was headed, were down a long, winding corridor, so he was quickly out of view of the minder. In fact he wasn't intending to use the toilet at all but walked straight past it, down a set of stairs and into a long passageway that led to a garage where one of the President's cars was housed, not a luxury car like all the others but just a standard saloon, with darkened windows. This was the exit that the President used for the nocturnal visits that he wanted kept secret. Saali pushed the garage door open and upwards. This way he was able to leave the Palace unseen. If he had tried to use one of the main entrances Basma would have been informed immediately but this way he bought a little time. Outside Saali waited in the shadows for a few minutes until his own car arrived, with Raffi at the wheel. The rendezvous had been the subject of the first of the two messages that Saali had sent. The second had been to General Hassan, Commander of the Fifth Regiment and an old friend. Hassan was the one leading member of the military that Saali knew he could trust. They were in agreement that Chafik should never be allowed to become president and had jointly decided on the course of action that should follow Baashir's death, although the general knew nothing of the manner of its cause. Hassan was to order his men to surround the palace and prevent anyone from leaving or entering. They were also to take control of the state broadcasting studios and other key buildings. His troops had already been put on high alert and moved towards the relevant vicinities. The text message was the order to move forward and also the instruction to start the movement of heavy artillery into the capital.

In the car Saali made several more calls. The first was to the Head of the State Broadcasting Service. Saali informed him of the President's death and told him to cancel all programming on the two state TV channels and on the radio and to put out martial music instead, with a notice that the Vice President would address the nation shortly. He was also told to have a studio prepared for that address. The next call was to the Chief of the General Staff (second to the President who was Commander in Chief). General Amir was also Head of the Presidential Bodyguard, although he had occupied both positions for only a few months as the President regularly shifted his generals from post to post to prevent any one becoming too powerful. This call was going to be tricky; Saali had not been able to establish any rapport with the man in his short time in post and he was concerned that he would protest the course of action that Saali would propose. That course was for the armed forces to be put on alert but remain in base until Saali gave further orders. The exception was the Fifth Regiment which had already been ordered to guard the palace and certain key buildings. As anticipated, General Amir expressed surprise, bordering on open anger, that the Fifth had been despatched to do what was obviously the Presidential Bodyguard's responsibility. Saali had to be reassuring but firm.

"Guarding the Palace is the least of our worries. I want you and your forces to be ready to react anywhere where there might be trouble. There are a lot of elements that might use the occasion of the President's death to provoke open revolt and uprising, especially out in the countryside where our hold is less secure. Your role will be vital if this should occur. In any case, it is my decision as Acting President. I also want you at the TV studio in one hour's time, to stand beside me as the oath is taken. That is only befitting the importance of your position."

Thus flattered, General Amir raised no further objections, although Saali knew that his compliance was not guaranteed; what Amir would do over the next day or two might prove crucial to the success or otherwise of his plans and Saali realised that it was significant that Amir had been at Chafik's side in the aftermath of the supposed terrorist episode.

The other calls were to various VIP's, the Speakers of the two Houses of Congress, the Head of the Supreme Court and religious leaders etc, informing them of the situation and requiring their company at the TV studio. One other message was contained in all these phone calls; the President's wife had requested to be allowed to grieve in private and neither she, nor any of her family were to be contacted.

Saali did not go directly to the studios. Instead he directed Raafi to take him to the mosque he sometimes used. There he joined in the Maghrib prayers held at sunset. It was not that Saali was particularly devout, more that he felt a particular need for observance after his actions that day. Besides, the hours after the sunset prayers would be when most people were at home, with the TV on and whilst any delay was fraught with danger, he didn't want to go on air too soon.

At the studios everything was prepared for the broadcast and all those instructed to attend were already there, with the exception of General Amir. Saali went straight into make-up, resolving to give Amir fifteen minutes before pressing ahead without him. In the event the General did not arrive, either before or after the broadcast. His absence was worrying.

Saali's speech had been prepared in advance. Although written down, he knew it by heart. It was brief and to the point.

"Fellow citizens, it is with deep regret that I have to inform you tonight of the death of His Excellency, Baashir al-Baqri, the President of the Republic. The President died peacefully at home in the presidential palace today, surrounded by his family. The cause of death was cancer, a condition that had been diagnosed over a year ago. Despite the best possible medical care, the condition gradually worsened. Although he fought against it bravely, the end, I'm afraid, was inevitable.

At this time of great national sadness you are requested to respect the family's need for privacy and, whilst grieving in private, to go about your daily business. Apart from the guarding of a few public buildings the army, whilst on alert, will remain in base. Shops, offices and other businesses are to remain open as usual until the day of the funeral, which will be a national day of mourning and the arrangements for which will be announced shortly.

As you know, the Constitution states that on the death of a president in office, the position passes to the person in the office of the vice president. While it is a position that I have never sought, it is a responsibility that I now reluctantly but dutifully accept, knowing at this difficult time, that the stability of the nation is of the utmost importance. I now call upon the Head of the Supreme Court to administer the oath of office."

At this point Saali rose to face the chief judge, raised his right hand and repeated the words:

"I, Saali al-Malimi, do solemnly affirm that I, according to the laws, shall faithfully discharge the functions of the office of the President. I shall possess pure faith and obedience to the State. I shall preserve, support and secure the constitution and I shall deal with all with equity as suggested by laws, without being affected by fear or mercy, love or hatred."

Then Saali shook hands with all those present and the station reverted to playing martial music, inserting a loop, every fifteen minutes, of Saali's announcement and the taking of the oath.

Saali didn't go home that night. The house was in a quiet suburban area and Saali feared it might be vulnerable should his plans backfire, so he had sent his sisters off to stay with an aunt in the countryside and booked himself into the Intercontinental Hotel. This was the capital's finest and also the main staying place for foreign journalists, visiting VIP's, officers of NGO's and the like. As such it was unlikely to be openly raided by the security forces. If necessary he could hole up there for some time.

After settling into his suite Saali ate in one of the hotel's restaurants, thus making sure that his presence was noted by the journalists there, although he fended off the barrage of questions he faced before his food arrived and he was allowed to eat in peace. While eating Saali noticed the vibrations on his phone and saw that Basma was calling. He ignored the calls but later, back in his suite, he phoned her. Basma was irate, demanding to know what game he was playing and why she was being imprisoned in her own home. Saali had anticipated this conversation and had already thought through his response. His intention was to stall and play for time, at least until after the funeral had taken place.

"Madam, nothing has changed, except that the death of the President means that we cannot transfer the vice presidency to Chafik immediately. That can only be done by the President...."

"But Chafik is to be the President, not Vice President."

"Yes, Madam, but we must follow the law. For Chafik

to become the President without being elected means that he must firstly become Vice President and then step into the President's shoes when he leaves office within his period of tenure. We must proceed according to the Constitution."

"So, you will appoint Chafik Vice President and then immediately stand down so he can take over?"

"That would look a little unseemly, Madam, especially so soon after Baashir's death when Chafik will be in mourning. Let's give it a little time, get the funeral over with and see how things settle down."

"And in the meantime Chafik is sidelined. I don't trust you, I don't think I have ever trusted you and why Baashir did, I can't imagine. You are up to something. Why did you sneak off like that and why is no-one allowed to come and go from the palace and why has the presidential bodyguard been replaced? It all smells of a trick."

"Madam, I can see that you're upset. It's only natural given the circumstances. Please allow me to answer. This afternoon, when Baashir died, I could see how devastated you were and simply thought it sensible to deal with the situation, with the technicalities, myself. There is such a lot to do at a time like this. I'm sorry I didn't consult you but I was upset too and just thought it best to leave without making a fuss. As to why I have placed the Fifth in position around the Palace, well it is simply that the Commander of the Fifth is the most professional general in the army. Anyone else might be tempted to use the situation to his own advantage but General Hassan can be trusted to do the right thing. Madam, we are in very treacherous waters. The death of the President may come as a surprise to the public but there are elements who have been waiting for this very moment to spring into action and who knows where the threat may come from. It could be from the right, the left, the Brotherhood, units within the army and, by the way, I don't trust General Amir one little bit, which is also why I wanted his forces away from the palace. He would have had you and Chafik at his mercy. And your personal safety, Madam, is of the utmost importance. I am not trying to be overly alarming but here are many elements that would be pleased to see you and Chafik out of the way. I am just trying to think of everything, to cover all eventualities. Now, we need to consider a lying in state and the funeral. Although it is the norm that funerals take place as soon as possible after death, the President's will have to be carefully organised with many dignitaries attending. With your permission I would like to arrange for a refrigerated casket to be sent to the palace and for Baashir to be transported to the Senate House for an official lying in state for twenty four hours, during which the public may visit to pay their respects and sign a book of commiseration. The day after that would be a good time for the funeral. Although we usually just use a white shroud, I think it would be more appropriate for someone as important as Baashir to be buried in a casket and for it to be as ornate as possible. The casket could then be transported, accompanied by mounted units through the streets to the National Cemetery. The actual funeral will be in private, in accordance with Baashir's wishes but afterwards there should be some kind of public event with VIPs, foreign dignitaries etc present and eulogies and speeches. With your permission, Madam, I will see to it all. We need to give him the best possible send off."

Basma didn't answer immediately but when she did it was with a tone of resignation in her voice.

"I suppose so. Just get on with it but be warned, no tricks or skulduggery. I am not without my own friends."

Saali was pleased with the conversation. He had conveyed to Basma that her own safety was not guaranteed, something which he doubted had ever crossed her mind and he had sowed the seeds of doubt in her mind about General Amir. Wherever he was and whatever his intentions, she would not be so open to any overture he might make. Most important of all, he seemed to have avoided a direct confrontation with Basma. He felt quite confident that she wouldn't cause any difficulties until after the funeral and he had his own plans for that.

EIGHT

When Nasir woke up, Samira was already out of bed. The sound of the television was coming from the lounge but Nasir's initial thoughts were about the passion of the previous night, the sort of passion he had never experienced with his wife. Presently Samira came in, wearing her dressing gown and carrying a coffee. She kissed him lightly on the forehead but did not smile.

"I'm sorry Nasir. You need to come and look at this, on the TV. It's not good."

It wasn't good at all. Nasir was the main news story. Somehow they had got hold of several photos of him. He was identified as the main author of an internet blog that had spread fake and slanderous news about the President's family in order to encourage dissent and revolution. Details were given about his job, his address and his family. Colleagues and neighbours were interviewed, some saying they had no idea about his activities, others that they had always suspected he was up to no good. The public were urged to report any sightings of him and to give any additional information they might have. The police and security forces were in the process of searching for him and were confident he would soon be apprehended and brought to justice.

Nasir didn't know what to say. He was just shocked.

"Saali has spoken to me already this morning. He says that he will sort it all out but you must stay here and not go outside at all until he says it's ok to do so. I'm sorry but they're expecting me back in the Special Zone. I have to leave now and I won't be back until Friday. There's plenty of food in the freezer and in the cupboards. Just help yourself to anything. I'll try to get a message to your wife and child that you're safe. It's better that you don't try to get in touch with them yourself; the authorities will be monitoring any calls they receive. I'm really sorry about all this. I can't begin to imagine how worrying it must be but you can depend on Saali. If he says he will get things sorted, then he will. It may take some time but you can be sure of it. In the meantime keep looking at the news; things are happening."

Samira moved closer to Nasir, put her arms around him, hugged him and kissed him on the lips.

"Last night was wonderful. I'm beginning to think you are a very special kind of person. Promise me you will just do as Saali says. That's the safest thing. Don't take any risks or do anything foolish. Just stay here. Saali will be true to his word; he always is. I have complete faith in him."

After she had gone, Nasir felt completely alone and

stranded. It was all too much to take in. It was if he was trapped in a whirlpool, being buffeted from every direction and gradually being sucked in further and there was nothing he could do about it. He was a marked man, a hunted man and if they caught up with him the outcome, sooner or later, would be his death. Samira said he had to trust Saali but his warning at the end of their meeting in the Special Zone kept coming back to him, 'You must understand, however, that if you are discovered and implicate me, I shall deny any involvement'. It wasn't only Saali he had doubts about. Could he really rely on Samira? Last night had been great but had it just been a cynical ploy to keep him onboard? If she was genuine then why was she so secretive? What had she got to hide? What was it between her and Saali?

Nasir's thoughts shifted on to Khalil and Aliyah. What would happen to them? Would they arrest Aliyah and torture her to try to discover his whereabouts? They already knew that the city home was empty and they would presume that she would know where he was. That she didn't might make the situation worse. The torture would go on for longer if they thought she was keeping the truth from them. And Khalil, he'd already seen his father violently seized and his mother assaulted in the process. How would he cope if he was now to see her being taken away? And what about all his plans for how the boy was to develop? That just looked impossible now, indeed the thought crossed Nasir's mind that Khalil might even grow up believing his father to be a criminal and a traitor. All these ideas kept going round and round in Nasir's mind until he felt he could scream.

After however long, he didn't know, Nasir tried to calm himself down. He took slow, deep breaths and tried to focus his thoughts on happy childhood memories. Somehow it worked. The sense of panic subsided. He made coffee, had breakfast, found some cd's and listened to music, western stuff, soft rock. Then he decided to find out if there was anything in the apartment that could tell him more about Samira and he spent many minutes going through every drawer, every shelf, every cupboard and every nook and cranny, looking for anything that might help. There was nothing, nothing at all, no letters, no photos, absolutely nothing personal. It struck Nasir that it was more like a hotel suite for her, than a home. You wouldn't find anything personal in a hotel room, it was just a place to stay for a day or two, not like a home.

Nasir turned on the television again. The panic returned. He was still there, the main news of the day. Even worse, there were pictures from outside the village home. Scenes of the police, all heavily armed, going in. The news reader said that the suspect's wife had been arrested. Nothing about Khalil. Nasir tried to think clearly. What should he do, what would it be best to do? To turn himself in would spare Aliyah any torture but it wasn't as simple as that. If he gave himself up they wouldn't simply bring a case against him and have him sentenced to death. They would want more information; who were his fellow conspirators, who had given him the information about Chafik and Basma? That would mean more torture, more of that sadist and that voice. It was not something he could go through again, the very thought of it was terrifying.

The only choices seemed to be to put his faith in Samira and Saali and stay put or to leave the apartment but if he did leave where could he go and who could he go to? Not his home in the city or to the village. Not the university either because they would be sure to be looking for him there and they would probably have the bus depot and the airport under surveillance too. He had friends yes, but to go to them would be to put them in danger as well. In any case, they had their own families to think of. They would probably not want to get involved. The others who contributed to the blog had doubtless gone into hiding already, fearful that they would be picked up. He didn't even know if it was safe to use his phone. He could think of no place where he would be safe, so if he did leave the apartment it would just be to wander around without purpose and risk being identified and reported. No, the only logical thing was to stay put and wait for Samira's call.

Thinking about the others on the blog made him remember the one the authorities had already picked up and who had given his name. She was called Ahed. They had known each other from their first day at university and had been quite close. He felt no bitterness towards her for naming him; indeed he imagined the torments she must have endured before giving in and answering their questions. If anything he felt remorse because she had not willingly accepted her part in his scheme in the first place and had only done so after considerable persuasion.

The day passed slowly. There were a few books but Nasir couldn't concentrate on reading. He kept the TV on, frequently turning to the main state channels and each time finding himself still the main news item. The rest of the time he flicked from channel to channel and in the end he just watched cartoons. In the afternoon Samira phoned, just a brief call just to ask if he was ok. She had nothing more to tell him and hadn't spoken to Saali since the early morning but he was to try not to worry and not to go outside. She would be back in a few days.

In the early evening the pictures on the state news channel suddenly want blank and it broadcast serious music instead. All the other stations were the same. Something was up and it had to be something important. The obvious thing was that the President was dead. After all, that's what all this was about, the President's cancer and imminent death and the need to prevent Chafik from coming to power. Nasir kept the TV on and waited, staring at the screen. The most immediate thought that came to mind was that if the President was dead and Saali, as Vice President, replaced him, then his ordeal might soon be over. Samira had said that Saali would 'sort things out'. It probably couldn't happen immediately, after all the new president was unlikely to start off by pardoning the person responsible for the blog that had put out so much critical information about his predecessor's family but after a few weeks, maybe Saali would come through for him. The other possibilities were all bad. Saali as President might turn out to be a rogue who had used him to further his own ambitions and who would then want him out of the way so that he would be unable to testify to Saali's contribution to the blog or that Saali might be intending to be only a caretaker president, before handing over to Chafik. Maybe Saali wouldn't become President at all and Chafik would take over immediately. Perhaps there was a power struggle going on between Saali and Chafik and who knows what the outcome of that would be.

There were so many possibilities, so many ifs and buts. In the end Nasir was taken by surprise when the picture suddenly came back and there was Saali, surrounded by the top brass, announcing the President's death and being sworn in himself. A few minutes later Samira called. Had he seen? No, she hadn't spoken to Saali and she didn't know anything else but it was good news. Saali had said he would help and now he was in the position to be able to do so. Nasir had to wait, be patient and not to do anything rash. He was safe where he was. She would be there again soon.

NINE

PRESIDENT SAALI AL-MALIMI made only one
announcement on his first full day in office and that was
to say that he had appointed General Hassan as Chief of
the General Staff in place of General Amir. The latter
was to keep command of his regiment. Saali knew that
Amir would be angered by this demotion and it was
difficult to predict what he would do about it but without
overall responsibility for the armed forces Amir would
not find it so easy to organise a military conspiracy
against him. General Hassan, on the other hand and in
his new position, would be able to keep tabs on Amir and
warn Saali of any untoward activity.

In the afternoon Saali visited the Senate house.
Baashir's refrigerated coffin was mounted on a dais that
was covered in purple velvet and guarded by four
soldiers. Saali peered into the coffin's glass window.
Baashir was dressed in his military uniform, complete
with the rows of medals he had awarded himself. Saali

had wondered how he would feel on seeing the body and knowing what he had done but Baashir looked at peace, almost serene. The undertaker had done a good job and Saali felt no remorse. Baashir was nearing his end anyway. On his way out Saali noticed how long the line of people queuing to pay their respects was. It stretched away into the distance. Had they all come willingly or had they thought it was the correct thing to be seen to have come? Saali guessed a bit of both; it was in his case.

The rest of the day was spent taking calls from home and abroad. Most of the internal ones were from ministers and officials, ostensibly congratulating him on his elevation to the presidency but in reality trying to find out if they were to continue in post or not. Saali prevaricated, saying that decisions had not yet been made. In fact the situation was rather chaotic since nobody really understood what was involved in a change of administration, as there had never been a change in administration since the overthrow of the monarchy. So members of the vice presidential staff were unsure whether they would move up with Saali or serve the next vice president, while the presidential staff were unsure of whether they would serve under Saali or be out of a job. Added to this was the complicating factor that everyone had understood that Chafik was to be the next president and nobody knew if Saali's appointment was temporary or not. Saali found it all rather amusing.

Some of these calls were from foreign embassies and consulates but a few foreign leaders or their underlings called him in person. These courtesy calls were rather tedious since they tended to be mostly the same in nature. The French Consul proved an exception, telling Saali that there had to be improvements in the human rights situation within the country for the flow of aid to continue and warning him of the need for free and fair elections, sooner rather than later, in order for his position to acquire legitimacy. Saali asked him if that meant that he had to allow the Brotherhood and various jihadist groups to be legalised and permitted to stand in these elections and got no firm answer. There were no calls from the USA or the UK, since both countries had broken off diplomatic relations some years before. Later, in the evening Saali phoned Samira to tell her that everything was running smoothly. Samira asked about Nasir's situation but Saali said he had to be patient. The first thing was to get the funeral out of the way and incidentally she should be sure to have the TV on for it and to listen to his speech because it was going to be rather sensational! Saali had prepared this speech some time previously and knew it off by heart. It was going to be very interesting to see Basma's reaction to it.

The funeral procession started at ten o'clock in the morning. Baashir's casket was mounted on an army gun carriage, pulled along by a single black stallion and flanked by a cavalry unit. The mourners followed on foot, Chafik and his mother first, then the other family members and then the dignitaries, including Saali. Basma and he had exchanged glances earlier but had not yet spoken. The general public followed behind. It took an hour to reach the cemetery. Some months beforehand

Basma had suggested that a mausoleum be built for Baashir but he had rejected the idea, insisting that he be buried, as was the custom, in a simple grave. Despite this Saali had arranged that the grave should be set aside from all others in an area of the cemetery that was as yet unused and which, after the funeral, would be cordoned off and beautified with lawn and planting. The actual ceremony was restricted to family, friends and a few important dignitaries. The public were kept away in an area outside the cemetery that had been prepared for the speeches that were to follow. Saali found the ceremony to be extremely moving; he had, after all, known Baashir since early childhood. He noticed that Chafik and Basma were both in tears for most of it. He guessed that Chafik's emotion was genuine but doubted whether Basma's was.

There were at least a dozen speakers before Saali, all basically extolling the virtues of the deceased president and expressing sympathy to the family. Saali was the last. As he mounted the podium and stood before the lectern a certain nervousness made him wonder if he would be able to remember everything he had prepared and he fumbled in his pocket for the paper copy. And, as he spread the sheets out, a doubt entered his mind as to whether this was the correct time and place to say what he intended. Perhaps not but he would say it anyway. He started by talking about the childhood he had shared with Baashir, including a few amusing anecdotes about games and tricks they had played, that brought smiles to the faces of the assembled and lightened the atmosphere. He talked about Baashir's strength in fighting the disease that ultimately killed him, how he was still alive months after the experts said he should be dead. Then he went on to talk about Baashir's ambitions for his presidency and for the country...

"He wanted to create a secular beacon that would be free of the corruption that categorises so much of the Middle East. A country that would be internationally respected. A country that would be transformed economically. In some ways he was very successful. When he became president most people lived in poverty, illiteracy was widespread, imports far exceeded exports. That has all changed. Poverty is much reduced. Literacy among the young is universal thanks to the state primary schools. There is a modern transport system and exports are booming and, as he said to me just a few days ago, 'This country stands on its own two feet now. The French, the Russians, the Americans, nobody controls us any more, nobody tells us what to do.' But the President also knew that his success was not complete and there was still much to do. He acknowledged this to me. 'I let myself', and he told me this himself not long ago, 'be too influenced by others and let them gain too much power. I knew that I had to rule with a rod of iron to begin with, in order to establish the Republic. There were many dangers, many enemies, many entrenched interests that worked against me, but I intended that rod to be temporary. Others urged me to make it permanent and I listened to them for too long. Now I think often of the dead and the broken and the bereaved and wonder how it might have been different if I had followed my own principles.'

At this point the atmosphere in the crowd changed. An intense silence fell, interrupted by one or two disapproving whistles. Saali persevered.

"I asked him once what he thought his greatest achievement was. He thought for a few seconds and said it was May 23rd, the date of the Revolution, the overthrow of the monarchy and the establishment of the Republic. Without that, he said, nothing that followed would have been possible. 'Success was far from guaranteed, there were so few of us,' he told me, 'I took my life in my hands but it had to be done. The King was a fool, a lapdog of the French and he was elderly. If he was bad enough though, then his eldest son was far worse, a moron, a womaniser, a spendthrift. That is why we had to overthrow the monarchy because in monarchies the eldest son inherits the country and we could not wait to let that happen. That is why we needed the Republic, because republics have presidents and presidents are elected. That is why May 23rd was my greatest achievement."'

There, he had said it. The crowd was silent but the meaning behind his words must have been apparent to everyone. He spoke a little more and then turned to retake his seat. He did not look directly at Basma but glancing momentarily he saw the look of venom on her face.

The following day was Friday and Saali had instructed General Hassan to put troops on standby in all the strategically important places in the capital and in one or two other important centres in case of trouble. There was none; Friday prayers passed off peacefully and there were no reports of disturbances anywhere. General Hassan reported however that Chafik had visited General Amir's headquarters immediately after the funeral and had spent over an hour there. No doubt they were discussing what to do in the light of Saali's speech. He had also had reports that Amir had been in contact with several mid-ranking officers outside his own regiment and wondered if Amir intended to set himself up as a latter day Nasser. Saali was not surprised. He had always known that displacing Chafik would be fraught with danger and that entrenched interests, Basma, her brothers, Chafik and those in their entourage would not take it all lying down. The next few days might prove decisive.

On Saturday a sand storm buffeted the country. It was so bad that power lines came down in various places, including the capital. Mobile phone signals were cut too. It suited Saali well, since most people had to basically stay indoors, cut off from communication with others. Sunday dawned sunny and calm. Saali had called a meeting of senior government ministers for 11am and put out an announcement that he would address the nation in the evening. Before any of that happened he took a call from Basma who was incandescent with rage. She accused him of treachery, treason and everything else under the sun. Saali listened to her patiently and, when she had finished her rant or, at least, paused for breath, simply told her that she had understood the situation perfectly and that he expected her to vacate the presidential palace within 48 hours and that he had instructed a removals company to remove her belongings to whatever address she wanted. A senior civil servant would visit shortly to establish those items in the palace that were state possessions and those that were her own and the family's and could be removed.

The morning meeting went well. Those who attended had understood his remarks at the funeral and no-one questioned his right to the presidency. Afterwards Saali had Raffi take him back to the hotel where he put the finishing touches to the speech he was going to give that evening. He called Samira and said that she should tell Nasir that his ordeal would soon be at an end. He also told her that everything they had worked towards was about to reach fruition and to join him at the television studios before his appearance. She should be dressed conservatively and have her hair covered.

The broadcast was due to go out at 8pm. Saali arrived at the studios an hour beforehand to go through last minute details and for make-up. There was a brief discussion about whether the speech should be pre-recorded or go out live. The director preferred to record it but Saali was quite confident that he could do it live and without mistakes; it was another speech that he knew by heart. He was also concerned that pre-recording it might allow news of what he had to say to get out, especially as he would be speaking before a small audience of invited journalists, and reduce the actual broadcast's impact.

Samira arrived a few minutes after him. She was smartly dressed but looked a little apprehensive and Saali spent a few minutes with her alone before she too went into make-up.

At 8 o'clock precisely all the country's main TV stations interrupted their programming to broadcast the President's speech.

"Fellow citizens, I stand before you as your President, a position I have never sought, nor ever thought I would attain. The constitution, however, is paramount and it states that on the death in office of the President, the Vice President must assume the role and this I am prepared to do in order to maintain continuity and avoid uncertainty that could lead to factional division and unrest. The present presidential term has just over one and a half years left to run and I intend to continue, God willing, in this role until the term is complete. I have made no decision as to whether I will be a candidate in the elections that will choose the next president. In the interim I intend to widen the field of possible candidates by allowing the formation of new political parties as long as they meet certain conditions in that this is a secular state, tolerant of all moderate religious opinion but opposed to religious and any other form of extremism. President Baashir was head of the ruling National Party but I have decided not to assume that role. This will allow the elections, whenever they come, to be more open and democratic. I have not yet decided on the person to be appointed as the new Vice President. That announcement will follow in due course.

This is a difficult time but while we mourn the death of the President, we must be aware that certain groups might wish to capitalise on the situation to undermine stability and promote factional strife. For this reason I have already appointed General Hassan, in whom I have complete trust and who has an unblemished record, as Chief of the General Staff, with orders to maintain a military presence in all places of strategic importance. There is no reason to feel alarm at the presence of soldiers on the street, they are there for your protection and it is only a temporary measure.

I intend the next few weeks and months to proceed as normally and for the transition of power to be as smooth as possible. For this reason I can confirm that all government ministers, with the exception of the Minister of the Interior, whom I have suspended pending a review of certain matters, will remain in their posts. This also applies to senior civil servants and members of the military. I am aware that the public is sometimes sceptical of the veracity of reports in the media, given the role of the government censor and to alleviate this I intend to relax some restrictions on the press and media so that reporting can become as objective and informative as possible and achieve the confidence of the public.

It is normal, in some countries, for an incoming or outgoing leader to pardon certain individuals of their wrongdoing and I intend to take this opportunity, with the exception of terrorism and the promotion of violence, to order the release from detention and prison all those charged or convicted of what are called 'political crimes'.

This will also apply to those currently wanted but not yet charged with relevant offences.

Every year an organisation called Transparency International publishes a list of countries starting with the least and finishing with the most corrupt. I am ashamed to say that this country comes far down this list. Fellow citizens, corruption is a curse, it deprives the state of revenues that would benefit all, it saps ambition and confidence and it undermines the rule of law. I am determined that the fight against corruption will be one of my administration's number one priorities. To this end I intend to make a start by ordering a review of all government contracts awarded in the last three years to see if they were conducted with due process and where anomalies are found, people will be called to account.

I have a little more to say but before that I am willing to take a few questions at this stage."

There was a slight awkward silence; the journalists present were not used to being able to question the President without first having their questions vetted and approved. After about twenty seconds one of them put his hand up and asked about the position of Chafik vis-a-vis the new administration. Saali answered that Chafik was a private citizen, albeit one with a high profile. He was not an office holder and was not being considered for any position within the new administration. If he wished to enter the political arena, he was perfectly entitled to do so and the public would form its own opinion. Saali then pointed to another journalist.

The second question concerned the person currently

being sought as the brains behind a certain blog and identified as Nasir Raziq. Was he included among the categories of people the President had said would be pardoned? Saali answered that Mr Raziq could not be pardoned as he had not been convicted but, yes, he would be a beneficiary of the amnesty. He was no longer on any wanted list and was free to go about his own business.

A further question concerned the Minister of the Interior. Why was he suspended from his position and what was the enquiry about. Saali paused for a moment and rubbed his chin before answering.

"This is a delicate situation. We are all aware of the terrorist incident a short while ago which ended with the deaths of the suspects in a disused warehouse. A few days ago it was suggested to me that the television cameras that covered the dramatic ending had been placed in position some hours beforehand, in fact before the initial incident that sparked the whole thing off. When I checked with the head of the television company concerned, he confirmed this and said that he had despatched the camera crew after being directed by the Minister of the Interior. I am sure that you can see the possible ramifications in all this, so I have ordered an enquiry. I make no prediction about its findings and outcome. It may be that the Minister will be reinstated, maybe not but we certainly need to get to the bottom of this."

Saali's answer provoked a flurry of raised hands, with journalists calling out but Saali remained calm and said that he would answer further questions on a later date but that he had one last announcement to make.

"As you know, I have never married, something I have at times regretted, and I live rather modestly, if I may say so myself, with my two elder sisters. As Vice President I had, of course, to attend various social and formal functions but never found these occasions to be particularly easy, too set in my ways maybe or perhaps it is that I am just no good at small talk, quite a shy person in fact, although you may not have noticed. Moving into the National Palace is not something I am looking forward to and my sisters have already told me that they flatly refuse to come with me. But move I must because of questions of security. And, of course, there will be many more formal and social occasions that I will be unable to avoid. What I am getting at is this, that for kings there is a queen and for presidents there is a first lady. And if anyone needs a first lady to share some of the burdens of office, it is me, especially as I am sure that none of you have noticed, I am not exactly a spring chicken any more. Well, I have found a first lady and wish to introduce her to you. She is a person, much younger than me, that I have known for all her life. In fact she is like a daughter to me, the daughter I never had. She is highly educated, a PhD in psychology and a university professor in France, although currently on a two year sabbatical. She is the daughter of the former president by his first wife and I wish to present her to you now as the new First Lady of the Republic, Samira Baashir Tariq al-Baqri."

Saali turned to welcome Samira into the room. She

came in, smiling and confident and stood beside Saali, saying nothing but with hand raised in acknowledgement of the polite applause that came from the assembled journalists. In fact all of them were trying to get their minds round the ramifications of what had just happened, completely unexpected as it was. Saali brought the proceedings to an end with a few more words, expressing the hope that he could win the confidence of the people though his actions as President and that he would always put their interests at the heart of his presidency. With that turned to look up to the flag of the country, saluted it, and then clutching Samira's arm, led her away and disappeared from view.

TEN

Nasir watched the funeral live on TV. Later on Samira arrived with more supplies and wine. This time their love making was more restrained, more gentle. Afterwards they talked but Samira was still reticent about revealing anything about her past, her parents, her relationship with Saali. It frustrated Nasir but he didn't press the subject. At some point Samira's phone rang. It was Saali. They spoke for some minutes and then Samira handed Nasir the phone.

"He wants to talk to you."

"Hello Nasir, I'm so pleased to have the opportunity to talk to you again. First of all I want to thank you for everything you have done. You put yourself under considerable risk for me and have suffered great hardship, not to speak of the terrible episode when you were tortured and beaten. It took great strength not to give away the details of where your information came from and for that I will be eternally grateful. The last few days must have been as equally difficult; seeing your face all over the media and having to go into hiding but I am happy to tell you, and this is the reason for my call that your plight will soon be over. I am addressing the nation on Sunday evening and I will be announcing an amnesty for some political prisoners, including those persons being sought but not yet under arrest and this will include you. On Monday morning you will be free to go about your business as usual. I expect they will make a big fuss of you at the university but please remember that my part in all this must never come to light. These are still difficult and dangerous times and it would add considerably to those dangers if it became known, how shall I put it, that I had been plotting against Chafik. Now, if there is nothing else, I will leave you in Samira's capable hands. I think she is becoming quite fond of you."

Samira didn't stay long. Yasmin's parents were away for the weekend and Samira was needed there. The next two days seemed to last an eternity as Nasir waited for Saali's TV address and to find out if he really would be freed from his situation. It also gave him time to think about all that had happened and to wonder about those caught up in it, his wife, Ahed and the others involved with the blog. They had to be at the top of his to do list after Sunday. Most of all though, he thought about Samira and whether they had a future together. For the rest of the time, there being nothing else to do, Nasir watched TV.

Samira arrived about an hour after the broadcast on Sunday evening. Nasir was not expecting her and didn't quite know how to receive her. After all, he had only just learnt that she was Baashir's daughter, the daughter of a tyrant, and that she was now the First Lady of the Republic. It was quite a lot to take in. Samira didn't say much to begin with, as if she didn't know quite what to say. She poured cold white wine for them both and started to fix something to eat. At last she began to explain.

"My father divorced my mother when I was only a few months old. I have never even met him in all the years since. At first he provided us with a villa in a nice part of town and paid for all our expenses. That all stopped when Basma found out. She insisted that he cut all ties with us. I know this because Saali has told me. He also told me that Baashir turned to him and asked him to look after us. He said he would pay him but Saali refused, saying that he wouldn't take anything. At this time Saali was working in a university in France but he came over quite frequently and I think that he and my mother developed quite an affection for each other. Nothing physical, I think, just a deep friendship. It wasn't that long after that life started to get very difficult. First of all there were phone calls, telling us we weren't wanted here and telling us to move away. These calls happened almost daily with a different voice each time and sounding ever more threatening, such as we had better get out or else something would happen to us. Then my mother was out walking one day, pushing me in a pram and a car swerved onto the pavement and came straight towards us. It veered away at the last moment so we were unharmed but my mother was very shaken up. She didn't know if it was just an accident where the driver had been careless and unintentionally mounted the pavement or if it had been deliberate, a sort of warning and linked to the phone calls. Then a few days later she came home from somewhere and found bullet holes in the wall outside. That couldn't have been an accident. My mother was really scared. She called Saali and he came straight away. He said that it must be all down to Basma, that she was capable of anything and that we should go with him to France. That's where we've been ever since. Saali set us up in a flat near his university where he lived on campus and looked after us. He put me through school and university and helped me get a job lecturing. I don't know what we'd have done without him. Even when he came over here to be Vice President he visited us regularly. He seemed to dote on us as the family he never had and he's like the father to me that Baashir should have been. I don't really hold it against Baashir, in fact I feel nothing for him, it's Basma who's caused all the trouble. Saali absolutely detests her. He blames her for stealing Baashir away from my mother and even more so, for corrupting him and turning him into a tyrant. He is absolutely determined to bring about her downfall and Chafik's too. Everyone knows that Chafik is totally unsuitable to be the president of anywhere. So to get rid of that possibility Saali knew that he would have to take on the presidency himself and that meant outfoxing Basma. He's been planning this for years, you know. As president he will be able, although it will be dangerous, to destroy what power she and her family retain and because I know that he is a good man, I'm sure that the country will flourish under him. I didn't really like the idea of First Lady but Saali was very keen. I think he thought that Basma would see it as the final humiliation so I agreed to go along with it. I got myself the two year sabbatical and came out here a few months ago on a false passport that Saali provided. He had the position for me in the Special Zone lined up and this flat as well and we just waited for Baashir to die so that everything could fall into place. That's it really. Now you know all about me. I'm sorry I couldn't tell you anything before. Saali said it had to be secret right up until the last minute. Only now it's suddenly become very complicated because of you."

Tears welled up in Samira's eyes and she suddenly looked distraught.

"I didn't contemplate that someone like you would come along. There have been men before, of course, but not anyone I felt for as much as I seem to be feeling for you. I think about you all the time and that's the problem because as First Lady I cannot be seen with anyone who is already married and especially not with you because if that happens then people will see a connection between you and me and Saali and they will put two and two together. And to make matters worse I am to have a personal bodyguard from tomorrow, so I don't see how we will ever be able to meet."

Samira pulled away and dabbed at her eyes.

"It's all come together perfectly for Saali, just as he planned but I just feel miserable. It's like I don't have any control over things any more. I wish I were back in France with my mother."

Nasir didn't know how to respond, so he said nothing, just hugged her. Later, after they had eaten and Samira was calmer they talked through the situation. That they had to stop seeing each other, at least for the time being, was obvious. About their future in the long run, they agreed that they would just have to wait and see. Samira said that she would go back to the Special Zone and live there for the time being; Saali wanted her to move into the palace whenever Basma and Chafik had been moved out. Nasir would go back to his place. Maybe there might be a possibility that they could use this apartment to meet up occasionally. Almost as an afterthought Samira reached into her handbag and took out a passport.

"It's for you. Saali thought you might need one if things go wrong."

ELEVEN

THE FOLLOWING MORNING, very early, Samira slipped out of bed, showered and dressed. Nasir was still asleep when she was ready to go and she left without waking him, deciding that goodbyes would be too difficult. Nasir stayed in the apartment, keeping out of sight for another two days, still not confident that the police would leave him alone. It was only on the second night when he saw footage on the TV of political detainees being released and interviewed that he decided it would be safe to go out. He left the apartment quite early the next day and made for his home. Out in the open he was still wary of being recognised and worried about what would happen if he was stopped by the police but the streets were still half deserted and no one gave him a second glance. He decided that it was safer to walk than to sit on a bus where people would have longer to look at him. Along the way he passed a newspaper kiosk and noticed his picture was still on one of the front pages. A little further on a general store was opening and Nasir went in and bought a pair of cheap sunglasses. That made him feel a little easier, a little less conspicuous. His walk was quite a long one. What was apparent as he went along was how much things had already changed. There was graffiti everywhere and all of it hostile to the Regime; the past president and the new one. In several places he saw the words 'The People Demand' scrawled on walls, shop windows and even on the sides of buses and where there had been statues of Baashir there were now piles of rubble. The huge picture of him that hung outside one of the municipal buildings had been defaced. His face now sported a Hitler moustache, his arm raised in a fascist salute. It was all rather thrilling.

Once back home Nasir made coffee and found something to eat. Then he made two phone calls. The first was to his wife's father. He expected another tirade but this time the man was very subdued. Aliyah had not returned after being detained, he was worried sick about her and feared the worst. Several policemen had raided the home, dragged the boy away from her and forcibly bundled her into a van. He presumed that she had been taken to the nearest police station but although he went often to enquire they would tell him nothing. He had listened to the new President's speech a few nights ago and would go again that day to tell them that his words applied to her and that she should be freed. If he came back alone, well they would both know what that would mean. In the meantime the boy was upset. After taking his mother away they had just left him there alone and terrified. Now he cried constantly for her and for his father too. Nothing he did seemed to comfort the boy; Nasir should come over as soon as possible. Nasir said he would call again later that day to find out if there was news of Aliyah but whatever transpired he promised that he would be there the next day. He finished by saying how sorry he was for all the distress he had caused. It was some minutes before Nasir felt sufficiently composed to make the second call.

That was to Ahed. Nasir, fearing the worse, didn't really expect her to be there but to his relief it was she who answered. She had been released late the previous night, apparently because of the new President's speech. She was all right, very shaken but all right. Her treatment had been bad. They had done things to her as a woman that she did not want to talk about but she was OK. She was sorry she had been weak and given his name and she asked his forgiveness.

"My forgiveness! You went through all that because of me and you ask for my forgiveness. It's me who needs to apologise for what I put you through."

"It's OK, Nasir. I didn't do it just for you. We both did what we felt we had to do for the country, not for ourselves or each other. It was for the country. I feel proud of what I did and you should too. Without you and maybe me as well that awful son might well be in charge today. We should meet up soon to celebrate but for now, just for now, I need some time on my own and with my family. You understand, I'm sure. I'll call in a few days."

Later that morning Nasir took his moped out and headed for the university. He wanted to find out about his job, whether he still had it and the extended hours he'd been given when it reopened. The university was spread out on the edge of town and comprised a relatively new but small, modern campus and several older buildings in a nearby residential area. Surprisingly it was the new buildings that looked the more run-down; they had been shoddily constructed and had soon begun to deteriorate. The admin building was in the new campus. As Nasir walked towards it he noticed students looking at him, recognising him, taking out cell phones, pointing him out to their friends. It made him feel uneasy and quite excited at the same time. The receptionist recognised him without asking his name, smiled and told him that the Dean, the head of the university, wanted to see him. His office was on the top floor. Nasir had never met the man and had no idea of what to expect, praise maybe or a telling down, perhaps the sack. The secretary told him that the Dean was occupied and that he should wait. She made him coffee without asking but said little. A few minutes later someone left the Dean's office and she told him to go in. The Dean was sitting at a big desk but rose, smiling and held out his hand when Nasir appeared. He was fat, almost bald and middle aged.

"My dear Mr Raziq, I'm so pleased to meet you. I was hoping you would be able to come. We are so proud of you and everything you've done. I expect the students will all be very excited. We had no idea until just a few days ago when you face was all over the media. Tell me about it. Has it been difficult, how did you get all that information? You must have had some high up contacts to be get hold of such explosive stuff. I'm sorry, I'm forgetting my manners, please sit down."

Nasir sat down, somewhat relieved. At least it didn't look like he was going to get the sack. The Dean was obviously excited to meet him. Nasir chose his words carefully.

"Yes, it has been difficult, being in hiding and fearing what would happen if they caught up with me. You may not be aware that they took me in a few weeks ago just because I was reported for speaking English to students in the cafeteria here? The torture was bad. I expect I'll always have the scars on my back. I'm sure you'll understand that my sources told me things on the basis of anonymity and I have to respect that, even now when the situation is different."

"But they must have been some very important people to be privy to such things?"

"As I said Sir, they have to remain anonymous."

"Yes, of course, forgive me. I don't mean to pry. It's interesting, that's all."

"You wanted to see me, Sir?"

"Yes, of course. I've been looking at your file. You teach the English Studies course and a few odds and ends to cover for absent staff."

"Yes, Sir."

"And, from what I gather people speak quite highly of you. Your head of department says you are diligent, your lectures are popular with the students."

"Thank you, Sir. I try to do my best."

"Well, given the importance of what you've done and what you've been through I've been thinking about what we can do for you, as a reward if you like. What I propose is that we give you tenure, take you on full time that is and what's more, at grade 2 level so that you'll get a decent salary. How does that sound?

Nasir couldn't help but smile. It was more than he ever imagined he would achieve.

"And looking at your file, I saw that your address is in District Eight. I hope you don't mind me saying but it is a very run down part of the city, an area where all the housing is below par. Given your salary up to now I'm not surprised that this is all you've been able to afford but after a few months on your new salary I'm sure you'll be able to get something more suitable. Until then, however, I have another suggestion. We have a number of apartments that are reserved for visiting speakers and other guests. As you probably know they are quite modern and well fitted out. You can have one rent free for the time being. I have the key here. The number is on the tag. Actually, one of the things that made me think of this is that your present home might not be safe. You are a hero to many but there are plenty of people who will be thinking the opposite. They might try to get at you. At the very least I expect that your present address will be besieged by reporters wanting an interview. They can be quite a nuisance. We'll make sure they don't know anything about the flat here and won't be able to bother you. What do you say?"

"What can I say but thank you? This is more than I could have dreamed of. You are very generous."

"It's the least we can do. You've done a great service to this country. We've all had our suspicions of course but now, because of you, everyone knows the truth about Chafik and his mother. Regardless of all the publicity regarding the terrorist or should I say so-called terrorist incident, I don't see how he can ever become president now and for that we are beholden to you. So, now we have a new president in the person of Mr al-Malimi, a rather controversial figure, I'm sure you'll agree. No one is quite sure about him. We can only hope that he proves to be a decent leader. At least he seems to be making the right noises now but then that tends to be how they all start off. We'll see. Time will tell. Go and have a look at the flat now and just hang on to the key if you want to take it. There are a few basic provisions in it. In the meantime I'm giving you special leave for the next week or so while we sort out a new timetable for you. My secretary has a cheque for you to tide you over. I'm here any time you need me. You don't need an appointment. It's been very good to meet you, Mr Raziq."

Nasir closed the door to the Dean's office feeling elated and immediately saw, through the window facing him, that the square below was filled with students, hundreds of them. When some of them spotted him looking down a great cheer went up. The secretary smiled as she handed him the cheque.

"Good luck with that lot down there."

Even before he was properly out of the building the crowd had surged forward and Nasir felt himself pressed in, jostled and then lifted onto someone's shoulders and carried into the surging mass of young people. The noise was tremendous. There was no way that anything he tried to say would be heard. Of course, it was rather thrilling to be the centre of so much attention, adoration even but it was also very disconcerting. Nasir felt that he had no control over the situation, no idea about what would happen next and it was also quite scary to be so precariously perched in the middle of such a melee. It went on for what seemed like ages. All the time he was carried around people were reaching up to touch him and to shake his hand. Eventually he was put down in the centre of the square where some steps led up to a plinth on which there had been, until a few days before, a statue of Baashir.

"Speech, speech," was the cry that went up and continued for at least a minute. At last the crown fell silent in anticipation.

Nasir had no idea what to say, of what they expected him to say. It was a situation that was entirely new to him. His mind was a blank.

As he hesitated a new cry went up, repeated and repeated.

"The People Demand the End of the Regime. The People Demand the End of the Regime."

It was Abdul, a friend of Nasir and fellow lecturer who came to his aid. He pushed through the crowd to reach Nasir, told him that there was to be a mass meeting later in the main lecture theatre and asked him to be on the panel. Nasir, seeing it as a way out of the current situation, readily agreed and Abdul, climbing onto the plinth, gestured to the crowd to be quiet and then announced the meeting, saying that Nasir would speak to them then. With that the students gradually dispersed.

"Thank you for that. I had no idea what to say."

"That's all right. I could see that you were floundering. It's not your everyday sort of situation is it? Can I buy you a coffee?"

"That's kind but I have things to attend to."

"But you will come to the meeting?"

"5.00pm, I'll be there.

Taking his leave, Nasir turned back towards the admin block and, once inside, asked if there was a back way out he could escape by. It had been a difficult few minutes. He'd never expected that sort of reception and he hadn't really enjoyed it. Once out of the campus he headed for home, stopping at a bank on the way to cash the cheque. As he turned the corner into his street he saw a crowd of people outside his house. After what the Dean had said he guessed they were reporters. He turned round and drove off, hoping he hadn't been spotted and wondering what to do next but then remembered the key he had in his pocket to the apartment at the university. Maybe he could get into that without being recognised.

The apartment was in a block in the modern campus

but away from the teaching areas. There was no one about. Inside it was small but perfectly adequate. Nasir was able to relax. He thought about what the coming meeting and what he would say about the country's future. He guessed that those attending would be fairly hostile to Saali and this placed him in a difficult position. He did not want to be too critical of the new president and, in the process, offend Samira but on the other hand, neither did he want to alienate the students. It would be a difficult balancing act. On top of everything he had never spoken to a mass gathering before and he didn't know if he could handle it. Just in case he found the situation too overwhelming and his nerves got the better of him, he spent an hour writing down his thoughts, trying to anticipate the range of questions that might be put to him.

The main lecture theatre was already packed when Nasir arrived there. In the antechamber behind coffee and drinks had been laid on. Nasir stuck to coffee, wary of the effect that even a beer might have. There were to be six other speakers on the platform, three lecturers, including Abdul and three students. The proceedings were to be chaired by one of the former students that Nasir had taught on his English Studies course and the two exchanged greetings and small talk before the meeting began. As Nasir stepped into the lecture theatre a wave of cheering broke out and as he took his seat the audience started shouting 'The People Demand' over and over. Nasir smiled and raised a hand to acknowledge the acclaim; inside it made him feel even more nervous. The chanting went on for some time before the place quietened down.

Once the chairman had introduced all the speakers, he asked each to make a statement about their views on the country's future. Nasir was the last. All the others made rousing speeches along the lines of how they were in the forefront of a revolution that would sweep away the old regime and usher in a glorious new age of freedom. It was just what the audience wanted to hear and they responded enthusiastically. When it came to Nasir's turn he basically repeated the answer that he had given Saali on that first meeting about wanting the country to move forward gradually and cautiously towards full democracy with universal suffrage, free elections, freedom of speech etc. It did not go down well. One of the audience interrupted him, standing up and shouting that gradual change was all well and good but how did that tally with bringing about an end of the Regime? It was not good enough. The Crafty One was now President, Chafik and his mother were still in the National Palace and even the new First Lady was the dictator's daughter. What he and everybody else wanted to know, was how to get rid of the lot of them. Should they take to the streets, maybe call for a general strike? What did he think they should do? Would he lead them? The interruption caused a general clamour. Most of the audience started to shout. It was impossible to make out what any one person was saying but the meaning was clear. They were united in wanting to bring down what remained of the Regime and their attention was focussed on Saali.

Nasir waited until the room quietened. He looked through his notes and then composed himself to speak. He knew it wouldn't be popular but felt it had to be said.

"When I started the blog,' he began, 'my intention was to bring to everyone's attention the reality of the Regime, to show how wicked and corrupt it was. That was something we all suspected, no not suspected, something we all knew to be true but the details were hidden from us by the mass media that was entirely in the hands of those in power. My blog was intended to break down that wall of secrecy and silence. Later my sources gave me insights into the truth about Chafik and his mother, shocking things that we had never even imagined. Our intention in making this public was clear. Sooner or later the tyrant would be dead and we wanted to make sure that his son could not inherit the crown. That would be something we would all be appalled by. Well, that has not happened. The Vice President has assumed the presidency. The question is whether or not this is just a continuation of the status quo and that Chafik will become the president in due course or whether it is a challenge to the status quo, a challenge against Chafik and his mother."

The audience was quiet, Nasir felt his nervousness slipping away, confidence in its place. He continued.

"One thing we need to be careful about is to avoid the making the same mistakes that happened elsewhere. In Iraq and Libya, for example, the regimes were swept away with nothing to replace them. What ensued was chaos and disaster, civil war, thousands, indeed millions displaced and the void filled with war lords and extremists, all intent in forcing themselves and their beliefs on everybody. We all know about the horrors inflicted by Daesh. In making our protest we need to be sure that the same thing doesn't happen here. We don't want to replace an evil regime with something even worse.

I want you to think about the present situation. For sure Saali al-Malimi was a stalwart of the old regime, someone much despised and known to everyone as the Crafty One but what has he done since the tyrant died? Well, first of all, I am here before you and able to speak openly, when just a couple of days ago I was in hiding and fearing for my life. He changed that and now myself and many more so-called dissidents are free and able to walk about in public. This was not something he had to do but he has done it and I am grateful. He has gone further, promising free elections and the formation of new political parties. This is to be welcomed. We all suspect that the so-called terrorist incident that made Chafik out to be a hero was a staged event. Al Malimi has announced an enquiry into it. Why would he do that, to find that it really did happen that way, that Chafik really is a hero? I think not; I believe that the enquiry will show Chafik to be the fraud that he is. So what is the conclusion that we should draw from all this? Well, for my part I think that a power struggle is taking place between the new president and the old one's family. At the tyrant's funeral al-Malimi said that in monarchies the eldest son inherits the throne but in republics it is the people who decide who their leader should be. Now, this might be a republic but we all know that Chafik, the eldest son, indeed the only son, was intended to be the next president. This has not happened and for this we have Mr al-Malimi to thank. None of us can tell what his long term intentions are and we have to be on our guard, to hold him to account but for me, for the time being, I'm willing to give him the benefit of the doubt. There is one other thing that gives me confidence in this. Who is the new First Lady? She is the daughter of the tyrant and his first wife. This might seem like a continuation of the old regime but it is not, it is a challenge to it. Can you imagine how insulted Basma must feel to find that she has been replaced as First Lady by the daughter of the wife she schemed against and replaced? It must be the ultimate indignation for her and it is another sign of a power struggle between al-Malimi and the tyrant's family. That is really all I have to say. It would be easy for me to stand before you and call for revolution and have us all take to the streets but that has never worked in this part of the world. Look at Egypt, the fall of Mubarak did not lead to a bright new beginning but to a new dictatorship and one that is just as bad if not worse than the one it replaced, the people still impoverished and denied justice. No, there is a new president here and he has been making all the right noises so far. I was told earlier today that they all start off that way, by making the right noises that is but who knows, at least he is making them. I do not want to disappoint you, to dampen your ardour for change but we have to be realistic about the present situation. The tyrant's family remain a threat, they still occupy the presidential palace but our best chance of removing them lies with Saali al-Malimi. I am sure this is not what you want or expected to hear but it is necessary that you hear it. That is all."

Nasir sat down to a silence that lasted for what seemed like ages, until the same person who had shouted at him before got up again.

"You can't be serious about this. The person responsible for telling us that The People Demand the End of the Regime is saying that we should just shut up and put up with its continuation, with the Crafty One as President and a daughter as First Lady. Surely you of all people cannot be telling us this. How much did they pay you to come out with this drivel? It's an insult to all of us. You ought to be ashamed. I'm not staying here to listen to this sort of rubbish."

With that, he stormed out of the theatre, calling out to the audience to follow. At least half of them went with him. The chairman tried to calm things down by asking the others on the platform what they thought of Nasir's ideas but, while none of them were openly condemnatory, neither would they come out in open support. When he asked for questions from the floor hardly anyone said anything, except one girl who said that none of them had been in hiding for their lives like Nasir and they had no right to criticise him for taking a cautious approach. Nobody spoke up to support her and with that the meeting came to an early finish.

Backstage Nasir was keen to get away but Abdul took him aside.

"You were quite right of course. Everything you said made sense, except this wasn't really the time or the place to say it. Sometimes you have to go with the flow."

Nasir felt like hitting him.

TWELVE

LATER THAT DAY Nasir tried calling Aliyah's father but couldn't get a connection. He tried several times, then looked up a weather forecast that told him of a sandstorm that was obviously interfering with the signal. It left him feeling even more worried and frustrated, given what had happened earlier in the lecture theatre. He wondered about the person who had shouted and then stormed out, whether he was justified, if he was right to be so critical. They had expected so much more of him than a defence of Saali. Then he remembered Saali's words at that first meeting, about how the country could never easily move from dictatorship to democracy, about how there was no experience of democracy in this part of the world and that there were too many people with entrenched interests in the status quo to allow that sort of change to happen. Saali had said that and now he seemed to be advocating the opposite, democracy, new political parties, freedom of the press, the very things he said could never happen. Was he being sincere or was it like the Dean had said, that they all start off making the right kind of noises before showing their real character? Maybe it was he who'd got it wrong, who'd been taken for a ride by Saali. These thoughts kept going round and round in Nasir's mind. Eventually, feeling hungry and remembering that the Dean had said there were a few supplies, he opened the fridge and found pitta, hummus and olives. There was also a bottle of wine. Nasir ignored the food and, as he had only done once before in his life, got blind drunk.

Next morning Nasir woke up on the sofa, still fully dressed, the empty wine bottle on the floor. There was nothing in the fridge, he had eaten everything, although he had no memory of it. His head ached as it had never done before. He showered and then got ready to go to the bus station to find a minibus to take him to his village. The walk and fresh air made him feel a little better but the trip in the hot and overcrowded vehicle was excruciating. His head seemed to explode with every little bump they went over and there were times when he felt he would have to ask the driver to stop and let him get out. Eventually he arrived.

It was Khalil who saw him first. He was playing in the street, saw his dad and came running and shouting. Nasir picked him up and kissed him over and over. Then he saw Aliyah. She had heard the commotion and come outside to find out what was happening. She smiled and came to him, then put her arms around him to hug him. Nasir was relieved to see her and a little puzzled, she had never been so openly affectionate before. Inside she made coffee and produced biscuits. When Nasir asked about her detention and release and whether she had been tortured, she grimaced. The worst part had been when they had come for her and dragged her out of the house and into the van. She had been scared for herself but more so for the boy. She had guessed it was the DSI and that she would be taken to the capital but they had taken her to a nearby town and deposited her at the local police station. She had heard them order the chief there to find out what she knew by any means available but when they had left the officer smiled at her and told her not to worry. It turned out that he had been an avid follower of the blog and was impressed to have the wife of the man behind it in his custody. He told her that she would have to be detained until he was authorised to release her but that she would not be harmed while in his custody. He would make excuses to the DSI. The previous day he had told her that the authorisation had come through and had driven her back home himself. So all in all it had not been too bad, except for the worry about Khalil. Nasir was relieved. His own experience of torture had been bad enough and he had been worried that she might have suffered because of him. Later she took him over to her father's, who also seemed to have changed his feelings towards him. He welcomed him back and said that he was proud to have him as a son in law. Nasir was slightly amazed and wondered if it was all too good to be true, especially her father's change of heart.

Having had no idea of what he would find at the village, even whether Aliyah was alive or dead, Nasir had

had no plans of what to do once he got there. It all depended on what he would find there. Seeing that the situation was as good as it was, he figured that he should go back to the capital that same day. Aliyah however would have none of it. After he had told her his side of the events, although he did not tell her anything about Samira and had to make up a few things about his hiding place, she said that he must stay, at least for a few days, in order to rest. In any case all the village wanted to meet him and they were sure to be invited around. In fact, Aliyah was like a different person towards him and it turned out that the police chief had told her all about his activities and how the country had so much to thank him for and how proud of him she must be. That afternoon she slaughtered a young goat and spit roasted it, saying that the situation deserved a special feast. Several of the neighbours came over, bringing salads and breads, to join the celebration. Fortunately, by then Nasir's hangover had gone and he was able to enjoy the meal and the accolades they laid on him. That evening, after Khalil was asleep and he prepared to sleep on the sofa, Aliyah took his hand and led him into the bedroom.

After the excitement of arrival it was only later that Nasir realised that they were in his old home. Aliyah had sent the tenant packing as quickly as possible and had already started to clean the place up. The following day he borrowed a moped in order to take her to the local town to buy paint and other necessities, When she came out dressed in a burka, Nasir told her to go back and take it off. He would not be seen with her in such a thing. To his surprise she did not object, nor did she say anything when he said that only her hair need be covered. When she appeared again she was still in black but with a smile on her face. The old Aliyah would never have done that he thought and wondered at the change that had come over her. She even walked by his side in the town and not three steps behind as she had always done before and she did it without him having to ask her.

Lying in bed that night, before falling asleep, Nasir's thought about Aliyah and Samira and how different they were. Samira, highly educated, refined, tall and thin, willowy even, with a classically beautiful face that was always perfectly made up. Her hair straight and falling to her shoulders or stretched tight and pinned at the back in a way which accentuated her facial features, her perfectly straight nose and narrow nostrils, the contours of her cheek, her long neck. Without her hijab she looked like a movie star, Angelina Jolie maybe. With it she somehow looked even more cultured. Even her voice was attractive with her speech taking on a slightly French accent. Aliyah was almost completely the opposite. She was small and full bodied, although not fat. Her face was rounded, her nose slightly aquiline and her hair shorter and quite curly. Her complexion was ruddy and she hardly ever wore make up. Barely literate, she had the look of the peasant about her especially in the dark, shapeless clothes she always wore. Yet there was a certain earthiness and attractiveness about her and when she smiled it seemed to light up her face. Perhaps however Nasir was noticing this because the Aliyah he had lived with in the city hardly ever smiled.

Nasir stayed three days. Together he and Aliyah set to work reviving the paintwork inside and later outside, pulling up weeds and trying to salvage what was left of the crops that had been neglected. They worked side by side, her chatting all the time, telling him all the local gossip, even laughing. Later in the day she made lovely meals with Khalil at her side, instructing him in the correct way of preparing this and that and fussing in a happy way when he got things wrong. The boy loved it and Nasir could see the strength of the bond between them. It made him question his plans to take Khalil away when he was of secondary school age and yet, if he didn't how could he grow into the modern person he so wanted him to become? It was all rather confusing. Nothing seemed straightforward any more. When it came to the time for departure, Aliyah and Khalil walked with him to the bus depot. There she thanked him for the money he had left her with her and told him to come again soon. Then she hugged him and told him that she wanted more children.

"Perhaps, in nine months you will be a father again," she whispered.

On the journey back to the capital Nasir thought about the situation. Everything seemed to be turning topsy-turvy. Samira, who had started out as a nanny, turned out to be a president's daughter and was now First Lady. Aliyah was being affectionate to him for the first time in their marriage and might be pregnant again, just when he had fallen for someone else and he himself had gone from being hero to villain in the eyes of the students in the course of a few hours. He wondered what sort of reception he would get back at the university and whether it might be best to stay away from it for as long as possible. In fact when he got to the apartment he found a letter waiting for him outlining his new duties. He was to give up the English Studies course and become a full time member of the faculty of Modern Languages, teaching languages combined with the study of areas of British, French and international history. He should use the rest of the semester to prepare for this and be ready to start teaching again at the start of the next one, some months away. It was quite a daunting task. In the meantime he was to receive the full salary of a lecturer, grade 2. The amount indicated seemed like a small fortune to him.

Samira called him three days later. She had been staying in the Special Zone but was going to use the apartment in the capital for the next couple of nights. She planned to arrive in the early evening. The bodyguard would only stay around until she had let herself into the apartment and she had given him the all clear. Once he was gone she would get in the car and pick him up in one of the streets near the complex and smuggle him in as she had done before. She was dying to see him again. Nasir was equally thrilled at the prospect, forgetting, for the time being at least, the changed situation with Aliyah.

He spent most of that day in the university library, preparing for one of his new courses but finished early in order to shower, change and get over to the part of town where Samira's apartment was. Once reunited they spent the evening eating, drinking, talking and making love, especially making love. In the early hours however, Nasir awoke and could not get back to sleep. He felt bad that he was there with Samira, when he had been with Aliyah just a few days earlier. He was deceiving both of them; Aliyah because he was being unfaithful to her, just at the time when she was more affectionate to him and Samira because he knew in his heart, that when it came to a decision, he had to choose Aliyah because of his son. His restlessness woke Samira and she sensed his tension. She asked what the matter was and when he didn't answer, she guessed it was something to do with his visit to Aliyah. When she pressed him, he tried to explain that Aliyah had changed and that he missed his Khalil. Samira said nothing but got up and dressed, told him that maybe they could talk sometime and then left. He heard nothing at all from her for several days but then, one afternoon, he got a call and she was so frantic that it was difficult to understand what she was saying. It took her several minutes to calm down sufficiently to explain.

THIRTEEN

GENERAL "FREDDIE" Amir was considering the way ahead. Until the death of President Baashir, less than a month previously, everything had been going to plan. At only forty years of age he had been the country's youngest ever Chief of Staff, if only to be stood down after five months by al-Malimi. Happily married with two young daughters, his wife came from one of the leading families, giving him many useful contacts. He was, he knew, a popular commander of his regiment and had gone to pains to socialize with the senior officers and to memorize the names and faces of every junior one. His own family was from the same clan as Baashir, a connection that his father had made full use of, rising to become a top regional administrator. It was his father who had him enrolled in the same American military academy that Chafik attended. He had told him to be sure to cultivate a friendship with Chafik; it would undoubtedly prove valuable in the future, as indeed it had. Freddie had been careful to maintain the friendship after Chafik had been sent down in disgrace, speaking on the phone often and, after his return to the country, meeting with him regularly to play tennis and golf but also carefully staying clear of Chafik's less respectable activities. His efforts had paid off. He had been a regular visitor at the palace, not only to meet with Chafik but also as a guest at various events where he mixed freely with the President and Basma. Through these connections he had been promoted through the officer ranks in super fast time and his appointment as Chief of Staff had been a natural progression.

Now all that hard effort was in jeopardy of coming to nothing. He had to hand it to al-Malimi; he had completely underestimated him. He had never for once given credence to the idea that al-Malimi might want the presidency for himself. Even on the evening of the President's death he had not thought it necessary to attend al-Malimi's swearing in and, until the address at the funeral, he had gone on believing that the office would swiftly be handed over to Chafik. He had probably destroyed any possibility that he might strike up a rapport with the new president and, what's more, there was the enquiry into the terrorist incident that was bound to conclude that the whole thing had been set up. That he had not gone into the warehouse with Chafik and had only been there to greet him when he came out with the three bodies, might be in his favour but the investigation might also find that he had been there hours earlier to check on the arrangements and that would surely mean the end of his career.

Already Chafik had met with him and phoned him repeatedly, imploring him to get things sorted and even threatening to take him down with him if the worst came to the worst. But sorting things out was never going to be easy. Al-Malimi was more devious and clever than he had ever imagined. He would undoubtedly be keeping tabs on his activities and had probably had his phones tapped. He might even have informants in the regimental compound. Also, he was close to General Hassan and there was no way of buying him off. So perhaps the best thing to do would be to ditch Chafik and try to ingratiate himself into the new reality. Maybe he could get al-Malimi to overlook his part in the incident and his long association with Chafik but how could he do that and why would al-Malimi play along?

There was an alternative, one that was infinitely more dangerous but one that would place him at the head of the armed forces again and as the right hand man of the President. That was to stick with Chafik and call upon his resources, certain junior army officers in particular, to help Chafik force al-Malimi from office. There were some people, some units on which he knew he could count. There had already been covert discussions. Not only that but there were many powerful people who had a lot to lose under the new situation. Chief among these were Basma's brothers but there were many others who had corruptly benefited under the old regime and who would almost certainly support him. The problem was how to galvanise all this potential support, how to arrange things in ways which could be kept secret, in effect how to organise a coup. Then an image came to mind of a shocking event that had been captured on film and shown on news programmes around the world. Maybe that was the way to do it.

President al-Malimi was also pondering the situation on that day. He wondered whether it might be expedient to reach some sort of compromise with General Amin in order to bring him onside or if it would be better to send him down with Chafik by revealing all the details of the fake terrorist incident. Not that Chafik was likely to take things lying down but separating the two would surely undermine their chances of mounting some sort of counter move. The more immediate problem however was that Chafik and his mother were still holed up in the palace. The people sent to take an inventory had twice been turned away. The brothers and many other hangers on had been in regular contact with them. No doubt they were making their own plans. It would, of course, be quite straightforward to storm the palace and have Basma and Chafik arrested but that would then necessitate a legal process that would take time and might provoke the enemy, those who had benefited under Baashir, to organise and fight back.

At length another possibility came to Saali's mind. He thought it through carefully and then placed a call to the palace, insisting that he only wanted to speak to Chafik because he guessed that Basma would reject his offer out of hand, while Chafik could be easily intimidated. Chafik answered. Saali explained to him that the results of the investigation had come through and that it was clear that the whole thing had been set up and that three innocent people had been killed in the process. He was considering whether to bring legal proceedings against him, including the possibility of a murder charge. Chafik started to stutter, blurting out that he had not personally killed them; that they were already dead when he arrived at the warehouse and that they were condemned to die anyway. Saali said the facts were clear, Chafik had gone into the warehouse, shots had been fired and he had come out with three bodies.

"Your family will lose everything if I allow this to go ahead. It is not only this incident that will lead to charges but also the many cases of blatant corruption that you, your mother and her brothers have been involved in for your own benefit. These have been documented, and the files are ready to go to court. There can only be one verdict. However, I am not a vindictive person. You have all been through a lot with the death of your father, who was such a dear friend to me and whom, I am sure, would not have wanted to see you suffer unnecessarily. So I have an alternative suggestion to put to you, a suggestion that would resolve the situation to everyone's benefit and without a messy court case that could only have one possible outcome. What I propose is that in return for my co-operation, and by that I mean hiding the report away and not initiating legal proceedings, you and your extended family will agree to go into permanent exile. I would organise an aircraft, a full sized jet, if necessary, for that purpose. I think that Qatar would be a sensible destination but it would be your choice. Moreover I would not be concerned about what you take with you, suitcases of dollars, jewels, whatever you have of value, so that you can continue to live an affluent life wherever you end up. Think about it please, talk it over with your mother and get back to me when you have decided. I think it is a very reasonable offer, in fact a very generous one considering the circumstances."

General Amir had to tell Chafik to calm down and start again. Saali had offered to drop everything if they agreed to go into exile. It wouldn't be too bad, certainly better than facing a murder charge but his mother was completely against the idea. What should he do? General Amir told him he would think about it and get back to him and as he did so it seemed to him that everything might be falling into place. He called Chafik back and told him to accept Saali's offer but to play for time, at least until after Armed Forces Day in the following week.

"And tell your mother not to worry. If my ideas go to plan you will all be able to stay here and you'll have the presidency as your father intended."

Chafik asked for details, how it could possibly be but Amir told him that it was better that no one else knew, including him. His mother would be sure to try to prize it out of him and then heaven knows who else she might tell. In the meantime they must behave as though they were going to leave, including the brothers and anyone else they might take with them. Order boxes, start packing, make sure documents were in order, that sort of thing. It would make Saali think that he'd got his way and he would be less suspicious, less on his guard.

FOURTEEN

President Saali al-Malimi was assassinated at the annual Armed Forces Day Parade along with General Hassan and two other leading generals. Armed Forces Day was a public holiday and a big national event. Thousands of people were ferried in each year from the outlying towns and villages to enhance the spectacle, enticed by the prospect of a small payment and free food. This year was no exception. A rostrum that could hold two hundred invited officials and other guests was positioned in front of a wide thoroughfare through which members of each regiment marched in strict formation, followed by tanks, heavy artillery and the special camel unit. On the other side of the thoroughfare was a line of stationary military lorries. Before the march past President al-Malimi, speaking from the top tier of the rostrum, made the usual patriotic speech, not even bothering to substantially change the words from what had been said in previous years. The climax of the afternoon was the fly past of planes of the country's air squadron. First came the six rather ancient jet fighters that had been purchased second hand off the French before the weapons embargo. They left vapour trails in the sky of the national colours and were followed a couple of minutes later by a fleet of slow moving military transports, engines roaring. For the duration of the flypast everyone on the rostrum had to look towards the aircraft and salute. That was the cue for three people, dressed as soldiers, in one of the stationary transports to leave their vehicle and run towards the rostrum, unnoticed by all except one. As they approached the rostrum they fired their automatic weapons into the top tier. President al-Malimi was hit by five bullets in the chest and died within minutes. General Hassan lived a little longer but was pronounced dead on arrival at hospital. While the firing took place the vehicle the assassins had come from, started up and drove towards them, picking them up and driving off at speed. Apart from this escape the whole scene was distinctly reminiscent of the assassination of President Anwar Sadat of Egypt some years earlier, indeed it was that assassination that had come to General Amir's mind when he had been thinking of ways to get rid of al-Malimi.

Amir had been on the top tier, along with the other generals, having had his first meeting with Saali since the death of Baashir. The President had commented that his presence had been sorely missed at and since the swearing in. Freddie had made rather feeble excuses but assured Saali of his loyalty. Then he made sure to position himself right at one end of the top row, near to the rear stairs that led down to the ground. While facing towards the sky for the fly past, his eyes were actually focussed downwards on the stationary transports and as he saw the assassins leave their vehicle and run towards the rostrum, he bent down low, pretending to adjust a shoelace, just in case. In the chaotic scene immediately after the shooting, while most people were frantically trying to get off the rostrum, he moved to the centre of the row and made sure that he was seen to try to aid the dying President. Only later did he leave the rostrum by the stairs and make his way to a waiting car that sped him directly to his headquarters.

The journey took only forty minutes; there was far less traffic than on a normal work day. As the car made its way through the half empty streets the General pondered on how well things had gone considering how fraught with danger the whole business had been, especially the clandestine meetings with the head of a local mafia outfit who was contracted to carry out the killing and provided with the necessary transport, uniforms and automatic weapons. That he had achieved all that without involving anyone in his regiment or any other spoke volumes of the extent of his contacts. So pleased he was that for a short while he wondered whether to change his plans and go directly to the national TV studios and declare himself President. He quickly dismissed the idea. Chafik would already be on his way there. He would claim the presidency and everyone would assume that the assassination had been his work. Only much later, perhaps a year or maybe more ahead, after Chafik had had plenty of time to demonstrate his arrogance, incompetence and savagery, did he intend to intervene to overthrow the new tyrant, portraying himself as the nation's saviour.

Once in his office Freddie turned on the TV to watch Chafik's address. It came on almost immediately, interrupting the martial music being played. That he was appearing so soon after the assassination would convince many as his complicity in it. Chafik had, in fact, suggested that this might be the case but Amir had persuaded him of the need to appear as soon as possible to prevent anyone else from trying to step in. He had only told Chafik the broad outline of what was to happen the day before and had insisted that he say nothing to his mother in case she decided to take control of the proceedings following the assassination. He told Chafik that it would be such a nice surprise for his mother to watch him assume the presidency and Chafik had stupidly agreed, saying it was a great idea.

Chafik looked distinctly nervous in front of the camera. Amir could tell he had been drinking and some of his words were slurred. He started off by saying that a terrible thing had happened that would unite the whole nation in grief and sorrow. He then explained for those who were not yet aware that the President had been assassinated earlier at the military parade to celebrate Armed Forces Day. The killers were undoubtedly jihadi extremists who were intent on bringing the country to its knees but that would not be allowed to happen. They would be hunted down and killed, just as he had hunted down and killed the terrorists in that earlier incident. He said that Saali al-Malimi had been a true patriot who had served the nation selflessly for many years and who had been a dear friend of his father, his mother and of himself. So close were they all that Saali was like a much loved uncle. It had been a great comfort to his father and to himself that he had been there to support him throughout his illness and even at the time of his death (this from the man who had given a telephone interview to a reporter two days before in which he had described Saali as a cockroach who had stolen the presidency and should be overthrown).

Chafik then explained why it was him speaking to the nation at this difficult time. He waved a piece of paper in front of the camera, which he said was an executive order that the President had signed that very day. It proclaimed him, Chafik, to be the country's Vice President. The President had intended to announce the appointment in his closing remarks at the end of the day's military parade. Of course, he had accepted the position, fully intending to support the President throughout the rest of his term of office. The situation had now, tragically, changed. While he had never sought the office of the presidency it was now his duty to step into that position as the constitution required. At this point Chafik abruptly stood up, taking the cameraman by surprise so that he only caught up with his face, some way through the oath of office which Chafik read out, proclaiming himself President.

Chafik concluded by asking people to remain calm. There would be a curfew from 6.00pm to 6.00am that night to keep troublemakers off the streets. Further announcements would follow concerning the arrangements for the funeral of the President and concerning whatever appointments he would be making to ensure that the good government of the country.

"It is an honour and a privilege to serve as your President. I promise that I will do everything in my power to discharge my duties honestly and effectively, to root out corruption and punish wrongdoers, so that the great people of this nation can flourish in the freedom from want and from oppression which they so richly deserve. God is most great."

General Amir was quite relieved when Chafik had finished and the station reverted to martial music. He had been increasingly concerned that Chafik, in his slightly inebriated state, might have forgotten his promise not to mention him. He didn't want there to be any indication that the two of them had in any way been acting together. To be reappointed as Head of the Armed Forces in the following days would be just one of the appointments that Chafik would be making. It wouldn't necessarily suggest any collusion between the two of them.

FIFTEEN

It took a little while for Nasir to understand what Samira was saying. It came as a total shock. He had not been paying attention to any of the events around Armed Forces Day. When he asked if there was anything he could do, she asked to see him and they agreed to meet a little later at his new place. He was in the university library when her call came and he went back to the apartment straight away in order to tidy things up. That done, he turned on the television to see what was happening. At first there was only martial music on every channel but quite soon that was interrupted by Chafik's appearance. Nasir watched in horror as Chafik declared himself President. The assassination was bad enough but this changed everything. Nasir realised immediately that he would be a wanted man again.

Samira arrived an hour or so later. She had dispensed with the bodyguard and driven herself from the Special Zone. As he opened the door to her she flung her arms around him and held him firmly for what seemed like minutes, not saying anything but weeping quietly. Nasir realised how distressed she must be. He said nothing, just holding her for comfort. Eventually she pulled away and said that she had been watching it on TV and it had all happened right in front of her eyes. It was like a scene from a movie but it wasn't a movie, it was real life and the person being murdered in front of her eyes was the man she thought of as her father, the one constant, apart from her mother, throughout her life,

She knew nothing about Chafik's pronouncement. When Nasir explained about it they both realised the ramifications. Nasir's life was certainly in danger and Samira's maybe. At the very least they would want to make her suffer. Her first reaction was to say that they had to get away, to leave the country as soon as possible. She took out her phone and called Yasmin's father in the Special Zone. He might be able to help. In between sobs, she explained the situation. Was there any thing he could do? It would certainly be safer in the Special Zone but she didn't want him to put him in any sort of danger. Yasmin's tutor, Nasir, he was with her. His position was even worse because of the blog. Could anything be done for Nasir as well?

When Samira finished the call she seemed a bit calmer. Yasmin's father would see what could be arranged. He would call her back as soon as he had anything. She was to try not to worry.

"Not to worry. How can I not worry? This is the

worst day of my life. Oh God, my mother, I wonder if she knows. It will hit her very hard. I have to call."

While Samira spoke to her mother, Nasir boiled the kettle and made mint tea. He wondered about Aliyah and if she was also in danger. Would they take her in again? Would it be the same friendly officer or would they take her to the capital and let that sadist loose on her to try to find out if she knew where he was. Maybe the right thing to do would be to turn himself in. That might mean they would leave Aliyah alone. Samira would have none of it. She seemed more in control after speaking to her mother.

"You giving yourself in would mean the death of you and it wouldn't necessarily help her. Remember that Baashir used to go after the whole extended family if he had a grudge against any one of them. It was both revenge and a warning to others to stay out of trouble because if you didn't, your loved ones are also in danger. Chafik will be just as bad, perhaps even worse because he won't have Saali at his side like Baashir did."

By then it was too close to the start of the curfew for Samira to get to the Special Zone or even to her own apartment. Nasir realised that she'd have to spend the night. With almost nothing in the fridge he needed to get to a shop quickly to get a few provisions. It would also give him the chance to try to think things out on his own. He was concerned that he might be recognised but the light was fading and he wore his sunglasses anyway. He walked to a street away from the campus and quickly filled a basket. The shopkeeper was reading one of his newspapers and took no interest in his customer. On his return he passed only one other person but crossed the road to avoid close contact. He got back just after the curfew had started but was no clearer in his mind of any course of action he should take.

Samira was watching television. The state controlled channel was repeatedly showing footage of the assassination and of Chafik's speech. An announcer said that the police and security forces were searching for the jihadis responsible and were monitoring any places where they might try to make an escape. The main airport was closed to all outgoing flights and bus terminals were also closing to conform with the curfew. Any members of the public who had any information should call a special number that was displayed at the bottom of the screen.

Nasir turned the TV off. There was no point in her repeatedly seeing what was so distressing. Instead he showed her the contents of his shopping bag and asked her to fix them something to eat. He thought it might take her mind off things a bit. Samira smiled and said she'd do her best. While she was peeling vegetables and opening tins her phone went. It was Yasmin's father. He had got them the last two places on a plane leaving the Special Zone's airport the following day at 10.00am. Earlier it had been only half full but after the assassination there had been a rush to get tickets by tourists anxious to get out of the country. He needed the details from their passports but he would only submit the information as late as possible. They should arrive at his villa by 9.00am and he would take them to the airport himself. Because of his position he hoped he would be able to get them straight onto the plane without the usual formalities. He thought it should all go well. He knew that the main airport had been closed but doubted whether the Special Zone's one would be affected. It was really only for tourists. The authorities would probably not have it in their sights.

The meal was good but Samira only poked at the food with her fork and ate little. Later she snuggled up to Nasir and talked about Saali and all he had done for her and her mother.

"I didn't speak any French when we first arrived there. He got me a personal tutor so I could catch up quickly. My mother was very homesick at first. She spoke a little French but not really enough to have a proper conversation, so he got her one as well and paid for it all. She was working in a pharmacy when she first met Baashir and to get her out of the house and to meet people, Saali got her a part time post in a chemist's near where we lived. She was there for years until her health began to deteriorate. She doesn't get about much now. Even after he became Vice President and had to move back home, Saali used to visit us often, at least ten times a year, sometimes more. Whenever and wherever he had to travel abroad for his work he would find time to stop off in Paris to see us. He always brought presents too. When we first moved to France he showed us all the sights of Paris. He took us up the Eiffel Tower and we were amazed at the view. One of the things I remember most is Notre Dame. I was only young and wasn't really interested, so after we'd seen the inside, he took me on the outside tour of the towers and roof. Mum stayed behind. All those steps took a lot of effort but I found it really exciting and more than a little scary to be so high up. I remember in particular getting so close to the gargoyles. Maybe I could take you there one day, that would be good."

Samira and Nasir slept together that night but there was no lovemaking; she just wanted to be close to him. When Samira finally got to sleep, Nasir lay there thinking. It would be so simple to leave with her. To be out of the country, out of danger. To live with her in France. Simple yes, but what about Aliyah and Khalil? Maybe he could send for them later but what if Chafik and his thugs got to them first, what if they used them to try to force him to return? There was another strain of thought as well. He was the person behind the blog. Others contributed but it was his idea; it was he who had organised it. What would people think if they were to learn that the author of the blog had fled the country at the earliest opportunity, to leave everyone else to face Chafik's revenge? Didn't he have a responsibility to stay and help, perhaps to lead the fight against Chafik, the fight against dictatorship and tyranny? Now was the time to act against Chafik, before he had entrenched his position and when he would be at his most vulnerable, not knowing on whom he could count, on who would support him or what the populace would do. All these thoughts and variations of them filled Nasir's mind for what seemed like ages. Eventually he fell asleep.

In the morning they drank coffee together and Nasir told Samira that he had decided to stay. She tried to persuade him against it but he had made up his mind. His duty lay there in the country. Was it her duty too, she asked but he said it was different for her. She was basically French; that was where her home was, where she had been brought up, where she had a job. She was only in the country because Saali had wanted it and now Saali was gone. Her mother needed her. There was no reason to stay.

Samira was ready just before 8.00am. There was no protracted farewell. She gathered up her things and just touched his lips with hers. Then she left the apartment and drove to the Special Zone. She had no problem getting in; the guard recognised her and opened the gate without asking her to stop. She sent a text message at 10.15am. She was on the plane, it was a little delayed but ready for takeoff. It was going to Munich. She wished he was with her.

Not long after Samira had gone there was a knock at the door. Fearing the worse Nasir did not answer it but then he heard a familiar voice, a voice that was not angry or threatening. The Dean had come to tell Nasir that he was sorry but he could no longer be employed. The situation had changed and his worse fears had come about. He had instructed his secretary to destroy any evidence that Nasir had been offered a lectureship. Ironically, he advised him to leave the country as soon as possible. They would be looking for him. He offered one crumb of relief. There was no record that he was living there. Officially it was empty, like all the other guest apartments. He could stay for a few days, maybe even a few weeks while he worked things out. He should be careful not to be seen coming and going and he should keep off the university campus because there would be spies about. Before leaving the Dean gave Nasir a wad of banknotes. His own money, not university funds. Not a great deal but it would keep him going for a little while. He hoped they would meet again someday, under better circumstances.

SIXTEEN

ALONE AGAIN, Nasir tried to think of what he should do. His first priority had to be the safety of Khalil and Aliyah. As far as he was aware only the Dean knew about the apartment so they would almost certainly be better off here than in the village. He called Aliyah's father and told him that they must get on the first bus to the capital. They should only bring a few essentials, enough for a few days. They should not go to the old home but meet him at a café that was near the bus station and that she had been to before. When they were on the bus he should text or call Nasir to tell him. That way Nasir would know when to be at the café. That was all he could tell him. It was important they came as soon as possible, before Chafik's men got to them.

Next, Nasir went to the nearest fleamarket, just a couple of minutes away and bought a second hand djellaba, slightly threadbare but with a hood, the sort of thing that poorer working men wore. He tried it on in the shop and kept it on. As he had only been seen in public before wearing western style clothes, Nasir thought that this would make him less conspicuous, especially with sunglasses. He might be able to move about more safely dressed like that. The shopkeeper looked at him quizzically and told him he looked familiar but Nasir said that sort of thing was always happening; he looked like someone on TV.

Back in the apartment Nasir fixed himself some breakfast and made more coffee. He turned on the TV but all the channels were still playing martial music, interspersed with the loop of Chafik's speech. The news ticker said that there would be important announcements later in the day. Aliyah's father called back around noon and said that Aliyah and Khalil were on the bus. It would arrive in an hour and twenty minutes, God willing. Nasir thanked him for his help. He hoped that things would get back to normal as soon as possible. He was glad the difficulties between them seemed to have gone.

The bus depot was quite a long walk away. Nasir left in good time. The streets were much quieter than normal, some shops were closed and boarded up, as if trouble was expected. There was less traffic on the roads too. People were obviously uncertain about the new situation, about what might happen in the coming days. Aliyah and Khalil were already there when he arrived. Neither of them recognised him as he approached and he had to throw back the hood and take off the glasses before Khalil screamed 'Daddy' and ran towards him. Nasir picked him up and hugged him. It was so good to see him again and have him there, with him. Aliyah waited patiently, just smiling. Nasir took her by the hand, saying nothing and led them both away, glancing around to see if anyone was following. Once into the back streets he slowed down, asked if she was ok and about the journey. She just grimaced and said they should talk later. When they got into the apartment Aliyah looked around in disbelief that Nasir could be living in somewhere so modern and clean. Nasir explained that it was only temporary, loaned by a friend because their home was bound to be watched and he had nowhere else to go.

It was difficult to talk frankly with Khalil there but later while he was watching cartoons, Aliyah whispered that she was scared and confused. She didn't understand what was happening and why she had to leave the village in such a hurry. Nasir explained the situation, that Chafik's men were sure to be looking for him and that they might try to use her to find out where he was. They might even use Khalil as well. They were safer with him. He didn't know how long it would last and he had no clear plan yet but he would try to think of something. She should try not to worry. He would look after them.

A little later Nasir suggested that she and Khalil go out to buy food. He didn't think that there would be a problem if they were out and about, their faces were not well known and anyway it would be something for them to do. Aliyah could also buy a few things to keep Khalil occupied; Nasir didn't want him just stuck in front of the TV all day. Aliyah gasped when he took out his wallet and she saw how full it was of banknotes. A gift from a friend, he said, the same one who lent the apartment. It was to tide him over. Then he told her he was no longer wanted at the university. There would be no more pay cheques and she should be careful not to spend too much.

When they were gone Nasir checked his phone for emails. A couple of junk mails that was all. Next he checked his Facebook page for the first time in days and was amazed at the number of friend requests. Then he looked at Twitter and found he had suddenly got several thousand followers. Obviously his newborn notoriety was responsible for the sudden interest in him. Nasir realised that some of these new followers would probably be bogus, people working for the new regime and that he needed to be cautious in dealing with any of them. One of the requests was from his friend Abdul. The photo confirmed it was him but to verify the identity Nasir used Facebook to message him and asked if he would relate what he had said to him after the meeting in the lecture theatre. A little while later Abdul replied, saying that he had agreed with what Nasir had said but had told him that it was not the place to have said it. He should have 'gone with the flow'. Nasir used the same cautious approach to make contact with several other people and in the conversations which folowed it became clear that the situation in the country was very tense. Sporadic outbursts of protest against Chafik's seizure of power were being put down savagely by the security forces, some of them wearing balaclavas to hide their identity and in khaki uniform that was neither regular military nor police issue. Even isolated individuals who tried to make personal statements against the situation, for instance by wring graffiti, were being brutally attacked. Nevertheless such protests were continuing and others, whilst not openly declaring defiance were making a point by keeping shops closed or staying off work. More than one of the people who Nasir contacted said that a coordinated approach was needed if the protests were to become more widespread and effective. Abdul was more frank. A leader was needed and Nasir should consider his own position. He was now a national figure and widely respected by everyone critical of the regime and of Chafik. Nasir could provide the leadership that could inspire hundreds of thousands to take to the streets. Nasir was non-committal in reply. It was something that needed serious consideration, not something to commit to without considering the ramifications for himself and for Aliyah and Khalil.

Aliyah looked pleased with herself when she and Khalil arrived back. Her shopping bag was full of groceries, enough to keep them going for several days. She was pleased but Nasir was worried; she had spent almost all the money he'd given her. Next time it would have to be a lot less. Still, it was good to see her happy and Khalil too. The boy delighted in showing him each of the toys that Aliyah had bought, although none were vaguely educational and there were no books to help with his reading. They were so different, he thought, himself and Aliyah.

Over the next few days Nasir was still unable to decide about Abdul's suggestion. Things on the street seemed to be getting quieter, more back to normal with fewer incidents of protest. Chafik addressed the nation on several occasions, always adopting a moderate tone. Some of his new appointments seemed to be widely acceptable, although, of course, Basma's reinstatement as First Lady was not popular. The latest announcement was that a referendum was to be called to confirm Chafik's position as president.

"Yes, and he'll win by 120 %," said Abdul. "We can't let ourselves be fooled by any of this. It's how they always start out, as Baashir did and like Mubarak did in Egypt, moderate at first but gradually turning the country into his own personal fiefdom, destroying human rights and suffocating any spark of personal freedom. We have to act now, while there is still time."

"What about Ali in France?" Nasir had said. "He's called for a general uprising to oust Chafik. We could get behind him."

Ali was a long term critic of Baashir. Abdul was scathing him.

"That creep, living in luxurious self-imposed exile in Paris all these years. Leaving others like you to face the danger here and carry on the fight. It's all very well for him to call for an uprising here but is he going to come back to lead it in person? Of course not, he'll claim the leadership but do it from the safety of a Paris armchair and if Chafik is overthrown, then you can bet that he'll fly back immediately to claim the credit. I wouldn't mind betting either that if he was to take over, he'd be just as bad as what's gone before. It's happened so many times all over the world, just like in Iran. No, we have to do it ourselves. You're the one, everyone knows about you. The blog has made you famous, that and the fact that they put your face on every TV screen and newspaper front page in the country when they found out it was you. You have to be the one to take the lead. They'll follow you."

"That's all very well but I've got a wife and child to think of. I can't afford to put them in danger."

"It seems to me they are already in danger. Your name is on the most wanted list again. They'll be looking for them too. Besides, we've all got family. We are all in hiding. Look, you don't have to do it in person, in public I mean, at least not at first. What about the blog, it hasn't appeared for weeks? Can't you get that going again or maybe use your Twitter account and Facebook page to start calling for action?"

It was what Abdul said about Aliyah and Khalil already being in danger that made Nasir decide. After all that was why he'd taken them away from the village, to prevent Aliyah being arrested. What would happen when the Dean told them that they must vacate the apartment, as he surely would and maybe sometime soon? Where would they go? How long would it be possible to remain in hiding and what sort of life was it anyway, not being able to go anywhere freely or to meet anyone? No, perhaps the situation they faced would only get better if Chafik was overthrown and if he had to play his part then so be it.

That evening Nasir edited his home pages on

Facebook and Twitter to show the photo of him that had been on wanted posters and newspapers and, after his name, he added the words 'The author of the blog, 'The People Demand the End of the Regime'. He then made several posts in which he reminded people of the various scandals that Chafik had been involved in and then detailed new ones that would have been on the next edition of the blog had Ahed not been arrested. These included new revelations of cocaine abuse and large payments to buy the silence of various unnamed women who Chafik had abused in some way. Nasir went further, saying that Chafik was totally unsuitable to hold any position of authority and that the people should resist him in whatever ways they could. He ridiculed the idea that al-Malimi had been in the process of making Chafik his Vice President and therefore next in line and said that Chafik had illegally seized the presidency. Nasir suggested that if people wanted to know the identity of the person or people behind the assassination of Saali al-Malimi, they should look at who had benefitted the most from it. A little later Nasir posted again that people should resist the new regime in whatever ways they could. That very night, taking advantage of the cover of darkness, they should make a start by putting up as much anti-Chafik graffiti as possible. Tomorrow they should take photos of it to upload onto social media.

Nasir said nothing about any this to Ayilah; he did not want her to worry. That evening, however, she expressed her frustration at their situation. Khalil should have been starting primary school that year and had nothing to do most of the time. He was soon bored with his new toys and missed his friends. She was also unhappy. Apart from a daily bit of shopping she had nothing to do. She missed her father and village life. She wanted to go home. The crops she had planted needed tending if they were to bear fruit in the coming months. Nasir explained that if she did go back, she was in danger of being arrested and tortured. He didn't want that and he didn't want Khalil to be around her when it happened. She had to be patient; she was safe where she was and the situation wouldn't last forever. Aliyah shrugged her shoulders and said nothing more. Nasir could tell that her newfound affection towards him was being put to the test and he doubted whether it would last. It made him think about Samira.

SEVENTEEN

THE GRAFFITI CAMPAIGN WORKED WELL. Very soon there was much more graffiti than the authorities could clear up. Nasir went out to see for himself, wearing his djellaba for disguise and surreptitiously taking photos on his phone to upload later. Many of the scrawlings were not just critical of Chafik and the regime but called for strikes, uprising and revolution and almost everywhere the words 'The People Demand' accompanied whatever had been written. Nasir was pleased but Abdul was unimpressed. Graffiti was all well and good, he said, but it was nothing new. They needed to occupy the streets, not just graffiti them. It was time to plan for the next stage.

It was about that time that things took an unexpected turn. A photo appeared on social media of a young man dead in the street. His face was badly disfigured. Very soon his name was posted. The authorities put out a statement saying that the person in question, Mustafa, was a local drug dealer who had been observed in the process of an 'unnatural act' with another man. The police had intervened to arrest them. One had run off but Mustafa in trying to escape had run into the path of an oncoming car and been killed. He had stumbled as the car approached and his head took the full brunt of the impact. The following day a video emerged of what really happened. The youth had been writing an anti-regime message on a store front window in broad daylight when he was spotted by two members of the security forces who proceeded to beat him up with such savagery that he collapsed and died. Even when he was clearly unconscious they continued to kick him in the head.

The video went viral. It even went international and caused spokesmen from several governments, including France, to call for a full investigation and for those responsible to be punished. Within the capital and in other centres the effect was electric and instantaneous. It was as if it was the final straw. Businesses closed, people came onto the street, crowds gathered, everyone demanding justice. Soon it became clear that the victim was no low-life drug dealer but a university student in the final year of a medical course and much praised by his lecturers, some of whom openly joined the protests. His imam said he was a good Muslim who did not take alcohol or drugs. The boy's father was interviewed, eyes watering and hardly able to contain his emotion, saying that the death of his son was bad enough but for the authorities to have concocted a story to destroy his character was unforgivable. He demanded that those responsible, not just those who had carried out the act but also those who had condoned it, be held to account. To make matters worse the Minister of Justice put out a statement saying that the incident had been investigated, the official story had been corroborated and that no further action was necessary.

Nasir messaged Abdul about the situation. They agreed to meet in a nearby park to work out a strategy. Nasir arrived very early in order to check out the location, just in case. They sat at opposite ends of a bench and talked, facing straight ahead and neither bent towards the other. Abdul suggested that they called for a Day of Rage after that week's Friday prayers. It would initially focus on bringing about justice for Mustafa but then develop into an all-out attack on the regime and Chafik. They should call for as many people as possible to gather in some location and then march to Independence Square and plan to stay there for as long as it took to bring down the government. Nasir approved of the Day of Rage but had his own thoughts on how it should happen.

"If we do it like that the authorities will just pack the route and the square with anti-riot police before we arrive. It would be better to suggest a different gathering point and then a march to somewhere like Maniq Square out on the outskirts. Given that we both have trusted contacts we could message them after Friday prayers to say there has been a change of plan. There is no gathering point and instead of Maniq Square people should go from wherever they are to Independence

Square. We'll ask the contacts to pass the message on to as many people as possible. What do you think?"

Abdul thought it was a good idea. If the authorities were expecting them to be elsewhere and had positioned their forces accordingly, they would stand more chance of being able to take control of Independence Square. They both realised, however, that taking the square would only be the start of it; they might have to be there for days, weeks even, before the regime crumbled and that would take a lot of organisation. They would need a committee to direct things. The two main entrances, the ones wide enough to allow cars and trucks through, would have to be barricaded. The many narrow alleyways that connected the square to the streets and souks beyond would have to be guarded. Anyone coming in would have to be searched and identity cards checked. Guns should not be allowed. They would need a myriad of things to see them through the days or weeks ahead, lights, generators, a loudspeaker system, food and drink. They should expect retaliation; the square was cobbled, the cobbles should be dug up, split if necessary to make missiles that could be thrown. People should come prepared for tear gas with swimming goggles or safety glasses for eye protection and face masks or scarves to cover mouths and noses. They should try to manage the flow of information and invite journalists in, especially from trusted sources like the BBC, Al Jazeera, Le Monde and France 24. They should invite prominent persons to join them too, politicians, writers, artists, business men and eminent people of every profession. They should encourage a cross section of the population to join in, not just young men. Women and children would be an asset; the regime would find it more difficult to order an attack on women and children. The role of the army would be crucial. The army was respected, not like the police and the security people. It should be encouraged to stay neutral. There was so much to think of, and to plan for and less than forty eight hours before Friday prayers. Nasir suggested that they use some of the time to try to find out as much as possible about what actually happened in Tahrir Square in Egypt. That way they would know what they might expect and be less likely to be taken by surprise.

Back in the apartment Nasir posted on social media, giving people the false information about when and where to gather and where they would march to. Very soon it was being widely repeated. There were many replies. Most just contained the words 'I'm going' or 'I'll be there' and things like that. Some trusted people were invited to join an organising committee once they had gathered in the square on Friday. Nasir also called on people in other cities and towns to organise their own Day of Rage. The more widespread the protests the more pressure it would put on the regime. That night Nasir hardly slept a wink. His mind was racing with thoughts about all the things that might happen. Above all there was the fear that the day would be a flop, hardly anyone would turn out and they could not get control of the square. If that happened he would be in more serious danger than ever before because of everything he was putting out on social media. In the end, unable to sleep, Nasir got up and watched TV.

Early on Thursday morning, before Aliyah was awake, Nasir called her father and they spoke for several minutes. He confirmed that security people had been several times, looking for Aliyah and that each time he had told them that they had gone to the capital and would most likely be at their home. Later on, partly because he could tell that Aliyah and Khalil were fed up and partly to try to take his mind off things, Nasir took them to a cinema that was showing the Disney film 'Frozen'. Khalil loved it, Aliyah too but Nasir could only think about what might happen the following day. Afterwards, instead of leading them straight back to the apartment, Nasir took them to the place he had met them a few days earlier. Aliyah was surprised and delighted to find her father there, waiting for them. At first she thought that he was going to take them back to the village but Nasir explained that he had come to stay with them for a few days. It would be a squeeze in the apartment but they could manage and he would be company for Aliyah. It was only later in the evening that he told them about the Day of Rage, the plans to occupy Independence Square and that he was one of the leaders of the protest. As such he would have to stay in the square for as long as it took. Her father could act as a go-between and bring him messages whenever they needed to communicate.

EIGHTEEN

INDEPENDENCE SQUARE WAS PRETTY MUCH in the centre of the capital. Not particularly large by some Middle Eastern standards, it could nevertheless hold several thousand people, maybe ten thousand at a pinch. One of its four sides was colonnaded. There were two entrances, wide enough for cars and trucks, at opposite ends of the square but there were several other narrower alleyways besides leading to the souks and roads beyond. Most of the buildings surrounding the square were single storey and of a similar Moorish style. In recent years some of these had been replaced with ugly, modern two or three storey blocks of offices and flats that looked completely out of place and spoiled the appearance of what had once been an elegant location. That said, quite a few of the older buildings were empty and becoming dilapidated. There were also gaps where the building had been pulled down to make way for a new development and which were now building sites full of construction material. Some of the remaining buildings that opened directly onto the square were cafés and restaurants, with outside tables and sunshades. There were also a couple of banks, some offices and quite a few mobile phone shops. Most of the shops selling the usual sort of tourist stuff had closed down in the past few years when much of the square had been dug up for the so-called archaeological excavations and tourists had largely stopped coming. These excavations had also put an end to the many market stalls and kebab stands that used to open every evening. Only a few had since returned. On the colonnaded side were several spice shops and grocers, although here again some premises were closed down. In the months since the excavations had ended and the diggings filled in, the cobbles had been replaced, although the surface was uneven and many of the cobbles loose. Some years previously the centre of the square had contained an impressive fountain. That had been replaced with a large square plinth, with three ascending levels, on the topmost of which was mounted a large statue of the dictator on horseback. The statue now lay in pieces on and around the plinth.

Near to the square were many of the buildings of state, the Ministry of the Interior, the Ministry of Information that also contained the news studios of the state run television and radio channels, the Ministry of Foreign Affairs and several others beside. This area also housed several foreign embassies and consulates and quite a few hotels, including the Intercontinental where Saali al-Malimi had been staying at the time of his assassination. Just a little further on, about a half a kilometre from the square, was the National Palace, set in its own elegantly lawned grounds and surrounded by high railings and by a recently installed electrified inner wire fence.

That week Friday prayers were due to finish between 11am and midday. Nasir made his way to the square and arrived around 12.15pm. It was already busier than usual, mostly with young men just milling around. He was wearing his djellaba and no one recognised him. There was no appreciable police presence. Abdul turned up a few minutes later and the two wandered around together, talking, waiting. By 2.00pm a fairly large crowd had gathered. One man came in pulling a cart that contained a sound system with mike, amp, big speakers and a long extension lead. It was what they had been waiting for. The extension lead was plugged into a socket in one of the shops where the owner was sympathetic to the cause. The sound system was set up on the central plinth. The crowd, now a couple of thousand strong, began to gather around, aware that something was going to happen.

Abdul and Nasir had already discussed and agreed on the approach they would take. They needed to occupy the attention those already there, while waiting for more to arrive. Abdul and others would do this by leading a series of chants. These would encourage a sense of unity and purpose. When enough people had gathered Abdul would pass the mike to Nasir to make the opening speech. Nasir knew the importance of this. As the author of the blog he was a celebrity, a symbol of opposition. The speech had to be inspirational. It had to set the tone to prepare the crowd for what was to follow. Abdul had arranged for it to be filmed and recorded so that in could be replayed at intervals and put out on social media. He told Nasir that he'd better make it a good one.

The chanting went on for about nearly an hour, "What do we want? Justice for Mustafa. When do we want it? Now." That sort of thing. Just as Abdul was about to hand over to Nasir a change came over the crowd as an elderly couple made their way to the centre and were helped onto the plinth. Mustafa's father, almost overcome with emotion that made it difficult for him to speak, thanked everyone for their support and said that Mustafa's death must not go unpunished. There must be justice for Mustafa. The crowd responded, chanting 'Justice for Mustafa,' over and over as the couple waved and were led away. This interruption hadn't been planned this but Nasir and Abdul could appreciate its effect in motivating the assembled throng.

The departure of Mustafa's parents was the signal for Nasir to speak. He mounted the plinth and stood before them. Then he threw off the djellaba and removed his sunglasses. It took only a few seconds for the crowd to recognise Nasir and begin to roar. Nasir started up the chant about Mustafa again and let it continue for some time. Then he motioned to them to be silent.

"Yes my friends, there must be justice for Mustafa who was so brutally murdered but Mustafa is only the latest in a long line of people who have been cut down by the regime. We all know people who have been taken away in the middle of the night, people who have been tortured, people who have been killed and whose bodies have been dumped in the road for all to see. We know about the DSI. We know about Number 42. We all know about the paid informers. We all know about the lies that are fed to us daily by the state controlled media. We know about the corruption, the millions that have been siphoned away. We have been living for too long under this tyranny. It has to end. You have come here today because you want it to end and you are brave because you know the risks that being here today involves but you are willing to take those risks because you are brave. You are brave, you are heroes and together we will bring an end to tyranny."

Nasir paused to get his breath and as he did so the gathered masses roared their approval.

"The tyrant is dead but the police still believe it is ok to beat an innocent man to death in broad daylight."

Nasir paused again and the crowd responded, venting their anger.

"The tyrant is dead but the authorities still believe it is ok to make up horrible lies about Mustafa."

Another pause, another roar from the crowd, even louder.

"The tyrant is dead but the Minister of the Interior believes it is ok to blatantly lie about the circumstances of Mustafa's death, when we have all seen the truth for ourselves."

Nasir paused again and continued to pause at the

end of every sentence and with each pause the crowd responded more vociferously.

"The tyrant is dead but murderers walk free... The tyrant is dead but nothing has changed... The tyrant is dead but the regime continues... The tyrant is dead but a new tyrant has taken his place, a tyrant who may turn out to be even worse than his father... A tyrant who has illegally stolen the presidency... A tyrant whose past is known to us all... Cocaine addiction, prostitutes, corruption, we know all about it... A Commander in Chief who was thrown out of two military academies and failed his military exams. We know all about him... We know all about the staged event when he was willing to take the lives of three innocent people to try to make himself look like a hero... We know all about him and we will not allow him to get away with it. The tyrant is dead but the regime lives on... The tyrant is dead but the old First Lady is the new First Lady... The constitutional Head of State is mown down in broad daylight because it benefits the regime. The regime lives on."

Nasir paused one last time. The crowd, angry and incensed, jeered and shouted for over a minute before Nasir beckoned them to be silent.

"Today is a day of rage for Mustafa but one day of rage is not enough. There must be days of rage, weeks of rage, maybe even months of rage until the regime has fallen. We have taken control of this square and we will not give it up until the regime has fallen. We are staying right here. We will organise, we will speak out, we will demand and we will defend this place until the regime falls. That is what we are here for. That is why you have come. The regime will fall. That is what we demand. What do we demand? We demand the end of the regime. What do we demand? We demand the end of the regime. What do the people demand? The People Demand the End of the Regime."

The people took up the chant and roared it back to him. The noise was tremendous but it wasn't just noise, it was an outpouring of passion. In those moments Nasir knew that he had done it. He felt the power of control, he had them in his hands, they would do whatever he asked of them. They were not just several thousand individuals; they had become a single body, a single consciousness. The regime would fall. It would fall because the people demanded it.

Abdul grinned and slapped him on the back as he stepped forward to take the mike. He continued the chant for some minutes before gesturing for them to be silent. Then he told them that they must organise, to be prepared for whatever the regime might try to throw at them. The first thing was to erect barricades at the two main entrances and to guard them. There was plenty of stuff in the building sites to use. He called for volunteers willing to do this to raise their hands and then told those who responded to start right away. Next he called for people to guard each of the narrower entrances. They must only allow people in who had identity cards that showed they were not in the police or security forces and they should not allow guns in; this had to be a peaceful protest. The authorities should not be provided with a reason to attack them. Next he asked for volunteers to dig up cobbles and stockpile them by the two main entrances. They would be a peaceful protest, he said, but if they were attacked they would defend themselves and with stones if necessary. He told them to film what was happening on their phones and to upload it onto social media and to send it to their friends and not just to their friends, to their fathers, their mothers, their elders, their teachers. He told them that it was not enough for them to be a gathering of young men, they must become a cross section of society; of men and women, young and old, rich and poor, the famous and the humble. That way they could not be ignored.

Abdul went on to say that if they were to keep control of the square they needed food and water, blankets, that sort of thing. He hoped that most people would be prepared to stay overnight but any that had to leave should return the next day with provisions and anything that would be useful. Each person should have something to protect their eyes against tear gas, swimming goggles would be ideal but any type of glasses would be better than nothing. They should have face coverings too to cover their mouths and long sleeved shirts, so that there was as little bare skin as possible. They must be prepared for whatever the authorities might throw at them. Lastly he told them that they must not become a rabble. They must be disciplined. Only a disciplined protest would bring down the regime. There must be no looting, no killing.

Abdul handed the mike to another to continue the

chanting and he and Nasir got down from the platform. Nasir suggested a coffee but Abdul had other plans. First he told those milling around to go and commandeer tables and chairs and to fetch as many pieces of railing that they could find. As these started to arrive a few minutes later he organised them into a command post at the base of the plinth, the railings being used to turn this into a separate space. He'd been to the square the previous day to check it out and make notes and next he produced a large map of it on which he had already marked and numbered all the ways in and out. Over the next hour he organised a rota of people to man all these entrances over the next twenty four hours, at least two people at each of the narrower ones on a two hour on, two off basis, three or four at the wider entrances and far greater numbers at the barricades. There was no problem in getting people to volunteer. Abdul explained to Nasir that this was not only a strategic necessity but it would also involve more people in active participation, rather than in just being there and that this in turn would strengthen their commitment to the cause. Next he had people go round to all the businesses in the square. The cafés were ordered to stay open and make their toilets available to all. All other businesses were to close and put up their shutters. Offices and apartment blocks must lock any doors opening onto the square; those inside would have to use the back entrances. Abdul, in fact, proved to be a master at organisation. It was he who had organised the sound system and later he would arrange for a powerful projector to be brought in so that TV and social media images could be projected onto walls, for all to see. In his rucksack he had a loudhailer for use around the square and even a fully charged power pack to recharge mobile phones. Most of these things had never even crossed Nasir's mind. He realised how lucky he was to have Abdul around.

At last, when Abdul was satisfied that enough had been done, the two of them repaired to one of the cafés. As they did so the crowd surged around them cheering, patting them on the back, showing their support. It took them several minutes to get through. The café owner gave them coffee and pastries and wouldn't accept any payment. He was a kindred spirit. Some of the other café owners were not so supportive. They resented having to stay open and were afraid that his might be taken by the authorities as support for the insurrection. A few tried to profit from it by upping their prices but were forced to lower them again when Abdul found out about it. Their particular café owner complained to them that the business next door, a stationer's, had been ransacked before it closed. Its entire stock of cardboard and felt pens had been stolen. Nasir felt slightly guilty and said that they would try to arrange payment in recompense but he also felt encouraged by the placards that had suddenly begun to emerge. Most said 'The People Demand the End of the Regime' or just 'The people demand'. On one someone had simply written 'Chafik must die'.

That first day was more successful than Nasir could have dreamed. The few police who had been in the square to begin with vanished away as the crowd gathered and no attempt was made by the authorities to invade the square or break up the proceedings. Only the occasional helicopter overhead showed them that they were being monitored and probably filmed. The call had not only been answered in the capital; uploads on YouTube and other social media showed footage of protests in several other towns and cities as well. By the evening the numbers in the square had swelled to the extent that movement about it was becoming difficult. Nevertheless people continued to arrive, including many women, some of them with children. A carnival atmosphere developed. A group of musicians took to the platform and played traditional music, followed by a rock group that played well known western songs. There was even a pair of jugglers. As darkness fell kebab sellers and the like arrived, their stalls being lifted over the barricades and the air soon filling with delicious aromas. Nasir's speech was replayed several times, always prompting another chorus of 'the people demand'. It was well after midnight before calm descended on Independence Square and those who remained tried to get some sleep.

Nasir slept fitfully. Someone had given him a couple of blankets but the night was cold and the cobbles uncomfortable. First thing in the morning he called Aliyah's father. He was unaware of the preceding day's events. The state run TV had not covered them at all and he had never used social media. Nasir told him about YouTube and how to get it on his phone. He spoke to Aliyah and Khalil. They both asked when he was coming back but all he could say was 'soon'. Shortly after that the internet was cut, not only in the capital but across the country. At least it showed that the authorities were taking them seriously.

The second day was more difficult than the first. There seemed to be a general realisation that the regime would not give in easily and that there would be many more uncomfortable nights ahead. A few people wandered away and did not return. At least coming and going was easy enough. Many people went into the narrow alleyways in search of something to eat and drink and nobody encountered any police. Nasir had a welcome surprise when Ahed appeared. It was the first time he had seen her for weeks and she looked none the worse for her ordeal. With her approval Nasir introduced her on the plinth and told the crowd of the vital role she had played in the blog. She in turn spoke of the dangers they had faced and the torture they had endured. She made Nasir pull up his shirt to show them the scars on his back. It was a stark reminder of the dangers everyone there faced.

It was well into the afternoon before the chanting started again and this seemed to raise spirits. They were further raised when several well known people arrived and addressed the crowd. One of these was a renowned poet, another a journalist for the state run news station. He announced that he had quit his job and would remain with them to the end. He also called on each and every one of his colleagues to do the same. Later on two of them answered his call. Despite all this a sombre mood prevailed and it was only after dark, when people lit fires and the air filled with the aroma of kebabs that the sense of carnival returned. Best of all perhaps was when Ali Tamimi, the most famous singer in the country and someone who had found worldwide fame, turned up and sang to them, encouraging people to join in the choruses. Since his songs were so well known virtually everyone was able to do so.

On the third morning Nasir slipped away, putting on his djellaba as he entered one of the alleyways. He needed to see Khalil to reassure him. Somehow the boy had become aware of what was happening and that his father was in danger. He had cried when they had spoken on the phone. Abdul was against him leaving but Nasir went anyway. Once out of the souk he was careful to avoid the main roads, taking the back streets instead. He saw only one policeman on the way but crossed over to avoid him. Khalil was overjoyed to see him but cried when he said it was time to leave. He stopped crying when Aliyah said that they might all go to the square later that day. Nasir would have objected but saw that the suggestion calmed the boy. He was also aware that he had called for women and older people to join in the protest. It would set a good example if he brought his own family to the square. Khalil did not want to wait for 'later that day'. If they were going to go they should all leave with Nasir. So it was that four of them set off, Nasir, Aliyah, her father and Khalil.

Nasir was away from the square for about three hours. During that time an encouraging development had taken place. A news team from Al Jazeera had arrived and started filming. Not only that but they informed the crowd that the Intercontinental Hotel was filling up with journalists from several countries. One of them was a famous BBC Middle East correspondent. It seemed that the protest was making the news around the world, even if the local media were deliberately avoiding it. That afternoon Nasir was interviewed on the plinth by one of the Al Jazeera reporters who said that he had almost single-handedly, through his blog, started a revolution. Nasir, of course, downplayed his role, saying that he was only one of the factors. Afterwards he was amazed at how easily he had handled the interview. A few weeks ago such a thing would have terrified him. He was pleased as well that the rest of the family were there to watch. Aliyah and Khalil beamed with pleasure, while her father slapped him on the back and said that Nasir would surely be president one day. The interview was shown not only on Al Jazeera's Middle East channels but on the European ones as well.

A little later came a less welcome development. Until then pretty much anyone could stand up on the plinth and speak to the people. Usually they just led a series of chants. This time the man at the microphone started to rant on about how, once the new tyrant was gone, they were going to establish a caliphate under strict sharia law and expel all non-believers from the country. Nasir pulled the mike on him as soon as he heard what was happening and they bundled the man off the plinth. Nasir told them to take his details, boot him out of the square and not allow him back in. Then he took the stage himself and told the people that what the man had said was untrue. Among them were people of many different faiths and denominations, all acting together. Their sole objective was to bring the regime to an end. After that it would be elections that would decide what sort of country they would become, not the dictates of fanatics. The speech drew loud cheers and was put out on all of the Al Jazeera channels. Late that afternoon Nasir received a phone call from Samira who had been watching the events in the square on her TV. By then Aliyah and the others had left for the apartment. He and Samira talked for some time.

Soon after dark two army tanks trundled through the streets and placed themselves in front of the barricades at the two main entrances to the square. No one, Nasir included, knew exactly what to make of it, whether they were there to just to guard the entrances or for a more sinister purpose. The crews opened up the hatches and sat on top of the tanks. They smiled and were friendly enough. When asked about their intentions they said they were just following orders and had no idea of what would come next. Not long afterwards a rumour quickly spread throughout the crowd. Chafik was to address the nation that evening. The rumour was quickly confirmed. The tyrant's son would speak at 8.00pm. The news was greeted with glee. Most of the people there expected Chafik to announce his resignation. They had won. It would soon be over. The regime was falling.

8.00pm came but Chafik did not. The room in the

palace from where the event was being televised was empty, except for a lectern placed on a small plinth, along with several microphones. The crowd in the square was strangely quiet. Hardly anyone spoke but their eyes were turned upwards to look at the wall of a two storey building which was being used as a screen on to which the scene inside the palace was being projected. The people waited uneasily, wondering about the delay and worrying. At about 8.20 the scene changed. Chafik came into the room wearing the uniform of Commander in Chief and accompanied by Basma and several others who stood behind as he took his place at the lectern. His speech was brief and to the point. He had been patient for long enough. The protesters were guilty of treason. They must abandon their actions immediately or face the consequences. He could not sit idly by and watch these cockroaches try to destroy this great country from within. Those protesting represented only the extremes of the population, communists, atheists, salafists, jihadis, homosexuals, deviants, outcasts. The good people, the backbone of the country had had enough. They were no longer willing to tolerate having their daily lives disrupted by the actions of a few misguided individuals. Independence Square and other centres of protest must be vacated by 11.00pm. Tanks guarding the entrances would withdraw to allow for a rapid evacuation. Those who left the square would be able to return to their homes unimpeded. Any that remained would face the full wrath of the state, the police, the internal security forces and, if necessary, the army. They would be responsible for their own dreadful fate. That was all.

As Chafik turned to step down and leave the room, the silence in Independence Square gave way to an explosion of shouting and hissing. It went on for some time, an outpouring of anger at what Chafik had said. Nasir, Abdul and the other leaders hastily discussed what their response should be and then Nasir spoke to the assembled mass. Revolutions, he told them, were never easy. They always involved danger. He had never expected that the regime would give in, just like that, without a fight. So now the climax was coming. If they prevailed the regime would fall. But he could not force anyone to stay. Everyone had a choice to make, everyone had different circumstances. Anyone who wanted to leave was free to go and should leave with pride at what they had achieved, pride in what they had been part of. No insults should be thrown at them. They were not cowards or they would not have been there in the first place. Those who remained must prepare to resist. The barricades must be strengthened. Every cobble remaining on the ground should be dug up and added to the stockpiles. People should text their friends, colleagues, anyone they knew. The call should go out for people to come and defend the revolution.

During the next several minutes about a quarter of the people slipped away but over the next couple of hours their number was easily matched by new arrivals. The call was being answered. During that time, the engines of the tanks at the main entrances started up, although they had been running for nearly an hour before the tanks began to withdraw. By then the stench of diesel fumes permeated the square and surrounding streets. 11.00pm came and went. There was no sign of any police or security force gathering outside the square and text messages being received inside it gave no indication of any such activity in the streets of the capital and other cities. Although there was certainly no carnival atmosphere in the square as there had been on previous nights, the tension began to ease. There was a general and growing feeling that there would not be an attack in the hours of darkness. They should get what rest they could and wait to see what tomorrow would bring.

Nasir and Abdul did not rest. They talked about strategies, of how to organise against attack. While they were talking a man approached carrying a rucksack out of which he took a screw topped bottle filled with liquid.

"I've got about forty of these almost ready to go. Just need the wicks. What do you think?"

Nasir understood immediately and reacted angrily.

"Molotov cocktails, no definitely not. We are a peaceful protest. We don't want violence and certainly not anyone burnt to death. Please take it away."

"Listen, nobody wants anyone dead but you have to be prepared. The way I see it the only way they can break us is if they bring down the barricades. With them up the only other ways through are so narrow that only one or two at a time can get in, so they have to smash the barricades first and they'll have to use something big to do that, tanks or earthmovers, JCB's, things like that and stones and rocks will be useless against that sort of power. These things would be useful. They might be able to stop them. I've a shop in the souk where I've been preparing them. I can get them here within minutes. Then, if they do attack the barricades we'll be ready for them. All we'll have to do is squeeze in the wicks soaked in paraffin and set them alight."

Nasir could see the reasoning behind what the man said. It was true that the barricades were the weak points. If they were pushed aside then the security forces could attack in strength. He consulted Abdul and they talked for a few seconds.

"What's in the bottles," asked Abdul.

"It's mainly petrol but with a little engine oil mixed in. The oil burns more slowly and sticks to surfaces. It makes them more likely to be effective against heavy machinery."

"And why paraffin, not petrol for the wicks?"

"It's not as instantly combustible like petrol. Less chance of the thing going off in your hand."

"How do you know all this?"

"You can find anything out these days on the internet. Listen we were all hoping that Chafik would give in tonight but that was always a long shot. Dictators don't give in without a fight. They will be heavily armed. We have to have something to fight back with. At least with these we stand a chance."

Nasir and Abdul talked again.

"Okay, we get your reasoning but it has to be our decision whether to use them or not. We don't want to give them an excuse for attacking us. We only use them in self defence when they attack the barricades,' said Abdul. 'Don't take them directly to the barricades. Bring them here where we can keep an eye on them until they're needed. Is that agreed? Do you need a hand to fetch them?"

"My brother is waiting back at shop. We can manage together. It's best if you don't know which shop it is. Not just you, I mean, we don't want anyone to know. We don't want to get raided. No names either. If you don't know, you can't tell. Sorry to be secretive but things could still go wrong."

The Molotovs arrived within a few minutes, together with a jerry can of paraffin and strips of linen cloth. More would be available if needed. The man who had made them only stayed long enough to see them safely stowed at the base of the plinth. Nasir and Abdul talked into the small hours, both of them too excited with anticipation to feel tired enough for sleep. They talked about many things, their hopes for the country and of their upbringings. Abdul's early years had been very different from Nasir's. While Nasir had been brought up in the rural heartland, his parents scraping just enough together to put him through a local secondary school, Abdul had grown up in the capital. His parents had been wealthy. His dad had owned the best supermarket, the one where the affluent people shopped. Abdul had been educated at the capital's finest private school. He had gone to university in Cairo. While he was there one of Basma's brothers made his father an offer he could not refuse; to sell him the supermarket for a nominal fee or have his family face the consequences. The supermarket was sold and Abdul's parents, together with his younger brothers and sisters, left the capital, eventually moving to France. They were there now. After graduating, Abdul ignored his father's advice to stay out of the country and returned, determined to play some part in the growing protest movement. He had been an ardent follower of the blog and had long desired to make contact with whoever was behind it. He had been thrilled to find it was one of his fellow lecturers and someone he already knew. Nasir had not disappointed him. He was rising to the occasion. They shared the same outlook, the same vision for the country. Together they would force Chafik to stand down.

NINETEEN

INSIDE THE PRESIDENTIAL PALACE, at around 11.00pm, Basma fumed. She had insisted that Chafik give the idiots in the square an ultimatum to get out or face the consequences but then he had failed to make the necessary preparations to force the protesters to leave. His excuse was that he thought they would disperse of their own accord on hearing his words. As usual, with her lazy son, she would have to do everything herself. She summoned the Head of the Armed Forces and the Minister of the Interior to meet her at 8.00am the following morning. General Amir was distinctly uneasy. He had watched Chafik's broadcast and worried that the army was going to be brought into the situation. Basma's summons seemed to confirm this to be the case and it was something that he definitely wanted to avoid. His plans all along had been to allow Chafik to damn himself in the eyes of the population and then intervene for the good of the country, making himself into a national hero in the process. If the army was now to be used to attack those in the square he would then, as the head of it, be viewed as Chafik's henchman instead. The more people who were killed in the process, the worse it would be. So far he had managed to keep the army out of it, apart from the tanks used to block the entrances to the square and those could easily be seen as defending, rather than threatening those in it. Chafik was easy to deal with. They had been friends for so long and Chafik seemed to have a childlike trust in him. Amir had told him that the army should be seen as neutral and that any action against the protesters should come from the Ministry of the Interior. It controlled the police and had its own anti riot squads. Chafik was easy to deal with but Basma was a different kettle of fish. She was used to getting her own way and she was clever with it, clever and ruthless. He needed to come up with a way of dealing with her.

At 7.45am General Amir arrived at the presidential palace. He was shown into an anteroom. The Minister of the Interior was already there. The two men chatted, the Minister seemingly excited at what they were going to be ordered to do. He was convinced that a successful crackdown would serve to strengthen his position so he was looking forward to it. General Amir only smiled, as if in agreement. At 9.00am exactly they were shown into one of the state rooms. As they did so Amir took out his mobile phone and started talking into it, trying to sound concerned. The state room was empty of people but seconds later Chafik and Basma arrived. They seated themselves in armchairs but Basma gave no indication that the others should do the same, even though there were seats available.

Chafik and his mother had just had an argument. He had expressed reservations about using force to end the protests. It might turn the people against him. Basma had insisted that it didn't matter what the people thought of him. Unless strong measures were used the protests would grow and could end up forcing him from office. Why couldn't he be more like his father? His father would have known what to do and done it without any qualms. Chafik wasn't there to be liked, he was there to rule. So he should grow up and act like a leader. She had summoned the two people who could bring the rebellion to an abrupt end and all he had to do was to tell them to get on with it by any method necessary. Between them they had the means to put on an overwhelming display of force. If that didn't deter the protesters then that force would have to be unleashed and the rebels annihilated. It was as simple as that.

As Chafik took his seat Amir could tell that he was nervous. He always was in his mother's presence. So was he; he had come up with a plan but it involved a big gamble. When Chafik cleared his throat as if about to speak, Amir made a hand gesture for him to wait and pointed at his phone as if the call was important and took priority. Basma glared at him in irritation but Amir continued to talk into phone.

"This is serious, I'll be with you as soon as I can. We have to nip this thing in the bud. Give me a few minutes."

Amir put the phone away and turned to Chafik.

"I'm sorry to butt in Sir but this is potentially very serious. I'm afraid that there might be a mutiny brewing in the army. The reports are a bit hazy but as far as I can tell some of the less senior officers in at least two regiments reacted badly to your broadcast last night. They are saying that the army should be above politics and do not want it to be used to put down the insurrection. There is talk of them disobeying if they are ordered to do so and they have been putting out feelers to gauge the opinions of other junior officers in other regiments. This is exactly the sort of situation that I fear could easily get out of hand, so it needs to be dealt with before it becomes any more serious. I can assure you both that I will get to the bottom of it but it may take a little time. So far I only have few names of those involved but I know there are others. With your permission Sir, I'll leave right away to make an immediate start in sorting this out. These troublemakers need to be dealt with before they do any more damage. I'll keep you informed of course. I'm sure the Minister here will be more than capable of carrying out whatever you want without me"

Avoiding eye contact with Basma, Amir looked directly at Chafik for a response and was not disappointed. Chafik spoke without consulting his mother, telling the general that this was the last thing they needed and that he should go straight away and do whatever was necessary. He had every confidence in him and his full support.

General Amir thanked Chafik, then immediately turned to leave the room. He was careful not to look at

Basma, half expecting her to order him to remain but she said nothing. Outside the room he smiled. He had taken them by surprise. The gamble had paid off. The army would not be turned against the people. His reputation would remain intact and maybe, just maybe, he might not have to wait a year or two before becoming the saviour of the nation. Events were moving. The situation was fluid and anything was possible.

TWENTY

Nasir was awake early. It was going to be a crunch day. If at the end of it, they were still there in command of the square then the regime's days might be numbered. He also knew that it was just as likely that the overwhelming power of the forces against them could prevail, the square emptied and the leaders of the protest be arrested or dead. Nasir thought about the latter possibility. His mind went back to the horror of torture and he could almost hear the sadist's voice telling him what horrors would be coming if he didn't cooperate. Death would be preferable to having to go through that again.

Abdul had been awake before dawn and gone off to fetch coffee. Nasir was glad of it but refused the pastries that Abdul offered; he was too tense for food. They had already made plans for the day. Nasir would stay there by the plinth, lead the crowd in chanting and broadcast information or instructions as necessary. Abdul would move around the perimeter of the square with his loudhailer.

Nasir checked his phone and found that the internet was on again. He didn't know if it was a good or bad sign but probably the latter, an indication that the regime was confident it could control the situation. Social media however showed that it wasn't just in the capital that people were protesting. Squares had been seized in several other towns and cities and there had been marches demanding change. Some of these had been met with violence, people had been killed but still the protests continued. It was encouraging. Abdul meanwhile used the internet to search for information on how best to use Molotov Cocktails and then selected several people to take them to the barricades.

Not long after it was fully light reports came in that security forces were massing outside the Ministry of the Interior, just a few streets away. They were dressed in black and with full anti-riot gear, perspex shields, face masks and hard helmets. They were armed with tear gas canisters, truncheons and rifles. Some of the rifles were for rubber bullets and some to fire the tear gas. The rest were loaded with live ammunition. Nasir got up on the plinth to warn the people of the impending attack, telling them to put on whatever protective gear they had brought with them. He called on those at the barricades to be brave but also to follow whatever instructions they were given. They would bear the brunt of the enemy's attack and must hold out. Then he started another round of chanting.

At that point several helicopters flew in and hovered over the square. They were low enough for their engines to drown out any noise coming from the crowd. Several people jumped onto the plinth and dragged Nasir off it, just in case there were snipers in the helicopters above. The eastern entrance to the square was nearest the Ministry of the Interior and it was there that the security forces were expected to make their assault. The first sign that the attack was coming was when a bulldozer came into view, trundling towards the barricade with its bucket up high to protect the windscreen and the driver. Following close behind were the massed ranks of the security forces. When the bulldozer was about a hundred metres away it gathered a little speed and its bucket was lowered. As it approached the jumbled barrier of the barricade, the security forces behind unleashed the first round of tear gas canisters, aiming high to land among the protesters behind it. This generated some panic but some brave souls stood their ground and even snatched up a few of the canisters to hurl them back. Those with the Molotovs had been instructed to wait for a signal and then to aim their missiles at the base of the bulldozer. The signal was given when the bulldozer was less than thirty feet away. There were two people for each Molotov, one to light the fuse, the other to throw it. Within seconds around eight missiles had been hurled over the barricade. Several hit the top of the bulldozer, exploding in a spectacular flash of fire, two missed completely but hit the first rank of the forces behind, sending them scattering backwards and two hit the base of the vehicle as intended. Immersed in an envelope of fire it shuddered to a halt a few feet away from the barricade. By some miracle the driver inside was able to escape the conflagration. The door was seen to open and someone leapt out. He must have been badly burned.

That was it. The security forces withdrew to a safe distance, the bulldozer burned until it was just a blackened mass of metal and some sort of order emerged in the square behind the barricade. There was much coughing and wheezing but the instruction to have eye and face protection meant that much of the worst effects of the gas had been avoided. Abdul, who had reached the barricade just before the attack, phoned Nasir to update him on the situation and Nasir, from the safety of the base of the plinth, told the crowd, shouting and with the amp turned up to maximum to make himself heard above the din of the helicopters, that the attack had been repelled. It caused much jubilation. Very shortly afterwards one of the helicopters seemed to judder in the air. Someone in the crowd had fired at it with a pistol that he had smuggled in despite the ban on guns. The helicopter veered and flew away. The others did too. It was only round one. Some in the crowd thought that they had won and that the enemy would give up but Nasir knew that more would follow. Next time the security forces would be better prepared, having learned from this experience.

It was at least two hours before the next attack. In the meantime both barricades were strengthened as much as possible and the wider alleyway entrances to the square were blocked with whatever materials could be found. The attack when it came was heralded again by the arrival of helicopters, much higher up this time to avoid bullets but with more serious intent. They dropped dozens of tear gas canisters causing panic and mayhem. Many people were overcome and with so little space in such a confined area there was no way of escaping the fumes. Several elderly people had heart attacks; three of them died. It was a blazing hot day. There was not a hint of a breeze in the square. The gas lingered.

This time it was the other barricade and a bigger bulldozer. It came forward at much greater speed, so that there was a terrific scramble to get off and away from the barricade. There was only time for a couple of Molotovs to be thrown which simply glanced off the bulldozer before it smashed into and through the barrier, scattering people before it. Dozens were unable to escape in time and were badly injured or crushed to death. It continued on its path, pushing the remnants of the barricade before it, until three men were able to jump up onto it from behind, drag the driver out and bring it to a halt. Then the unexpected, the unpredictable happened. One of those who had jumped onboard was an experienced bulldozer driver. He turned the vehicle round and drove it towards and through the remains of the barricade and into the path of the security forces that were about to enter the square. The street was just wide enough for most of them to avoid the bulldozer so the carnage was not as horrific as it might have been. Even so scores of them were hit as the driver accelerated the vehicle. Many died on the spot and some later in hospital. Once the driver had gone past the forces he turned into a side street, stopped the vehicle, got out and escaped into an alleyway. He made it back into the square completely unscathed. By that time the security forces, in total disarray because of his prompt action, had given up any thought of attack. Most of them were wandering about in shock or desperately trying to help the injured.

While the attack had failed the situation in the square was chaotic. Despite the precautions against it, many people were suffering from the effects of the tear gas. People were running this way and that, many gasping for air, eyes streaming. The situation was made worse by people tripping over others who had already fallen to the ground. Many people tried to get away through the narrower exits causing a crush in which several people died. The noise of the helicopter engines added to the chaos, drowning out the instructions being desperately given out on the plinth. Nasir himself only became aware of the carnage at the barricade after many minutes. Himself coughing and spluttering he put out a message on social media calling for doctors and medics to urgently come to tend the wounded. Eventually, at least a quarter of an hour after the onslaught, the helicopters flew away and some sort of order returned.

TWENTY-ONE

General Amir came away from the palace and thought about what might happen next. The best outcome would be for the Interior Ministry forces to succeed in taking over the square and ending the protest there. That would allow him to proceed with his long term plan to give Chafik long enough in office to damn himself in the eyes of the people and then to intervene to overthrow him and become the peoples' champion. Whatever the security forces did that day would help the process of demonising Chafik and, from his point of view, the worse their actions the better. If, on the other hand, the security forces were unable put down the protest then he knew that the army would eventually be called upon to do it and this he could not countenance because it would condemn him in the eyes of the people. He had gained a little time by walking out of the meeting but that was all. If the order still came to intervene then he would have to refuse it and that was something which was fraught with danger. He would have to take the army or at least a considerable part of it with him or face arrest and execution. Yet the support of the army was not something he was confident about. He was its head but that didn't count for much because he was young and relatively inexperienced. He hadn't yet had the opportunity to demonstrate his authority by presiding over a meeting of the General Command because such meetings had to be called by the President and Baashir had been too ill to call one in the preceding months. He guessed that several commanders resented his rapid rise to power and he was pretty sure that some, indeed most of them would side with Chafik if called to choose between the President and mutiny. It was in the more junior officers that he had the greatest hope. Some of them would be idealistic. Some would be against Chafik on principal because of his past history and his illegal seizure of the presidency. Being young they would be more likely to be willing to take a risk; they had less to lose than established generals. He had already been making soundings and had the names of several young officers in various regiments who might be prepared to act.

Back in his headquarters Amir called for his senior adjutant, a man of wide experience and on whose loyalty he was sure he could count. He explained the situation and what he proposed to do and asked for his opinion. When the adjutant assured him of his support Amir told him to contact the young officers and tell them to report there for a meeting at 1.00pm. They were not to disclose the meeting to their senior officers and not to attend if it might arouse suspicion. The adjutant was also to make discreet enquiries to try to find out if there were any other like-minded officers.

Later on Amir turned on Al Jazeera. It was reporting on the attack on the first barricade and included scenes uploaded on social media. The protesters were obviously well organised. The barricade was well built, the Molotov Cocktails effective. He half expected a phone call from Chafik but none came. Shortly before the second attack the adjutant returned with the names of three more officers who were known to sympathise with the protesters and, what is more, were suspected as being part of a conspiracy against Chafik. Apparently there actually was widespread disgruntlement among junior officers in several regiments that Chafik had seized the presidency. It was more than Amin had dared to hope for and, rather amusingly, it confirmed the story that he had invented and told Chafik only hours beforehand.

Al Jazeera reported on the second assault. Scenes showed the immediate aftermath of the gas attack from above, as well as the bulldozer crashing through the barricade. Viewers were spared from seeing the worst of the carnage but this was readily available on social media. The studio commentator made the point that the use of helicopters to drop tear gas was unprecedented. International law allowed for it to be used as a crowd control measure but this clearly went beyond that. Being dropped by helicopter on a crowd trapped in an enclosed space might be seen as breaking international law. It could be construed as a war crime. Amir seized on that the last point. He guessed that it would be picked up by many other media outlets. It might go all round the world. The U.N. might even get involved. It would provide justification if he did carry out his plan to act against Chafik.

Just before the officers were due to arrive Amir received a call from Basma. She was fuming.

"At your service, Madam. What can I do for you?"

"The idiot in charge of the Interior has messed things up. Did you see the pictures? We have just had a call from the French Foreign Minister who is threatening sanctions. We need to get the situation in the square under control. I want the army to be sent in immediately. Right away, do you hear and make sure that you do it properly, no helicopters dropping tear gas or anything stupid like that. An overwhelming show of force is necessary if we are to end the protest without more unnecessary carnage and more phone calls from abroad. Get on with it."

General Amir was pleased that he was talking to Basma and not Chafik. It made what he said next easier.

"Of course, Madam, when I receive such an order directly from the President I shall act upon it."

"The President is indisposed. I'm ordering you."

Amir guessed that Chafik was drunk or stoned. It would probably be hours before he was sober enough to speak in person.

"Madam, with all due respect, you hold no official governmental position. If the President is indisposed I will have to wait until he is, how shall I put it, disposed, yes disposed, before I can take any action."

"Do not be impertinent with me. I'm not used to having my orders ignored, just get on with it."

"I assure you Madam, I'm not being impertinent, accidentally or deliberately, just following proper procedure. Such an order must come directly from the President himself. Please ask Chafik to call me."

The line went dead. He could only imagine how angry she must be and how useful it was that Chafik was not available.

At one o'clock exactly the adjutant ushered in about seven young officers. None of them looked older than thirty. Each was smartly dressed in uniform and each looked distinctly nervous. Only one of them, the officer in his own regiment, was known to him personally. Amir beckoned them to be seated opposite him at the large table that served as his desk.

"Good afternoon gentleman, there is no time for niceties; this is a critical moment so I must get to the point immediately. I have received reports that each of you is sympathetic to the demands and actions of the protesters in Independence Square."

There was no verbal response but they looked at each other apprehensively and avoided eye contact with him.

"You have seen the Al Jazeera pictures of today's events?"

Each of them nodded.

"Then I hope that each of you is as disgusted as I am, ashamed even, that actions amounting to war crimes have been committed against our own citizens. Within the next few hours I expect to be ordered to send the army into the square, something in all consciousness that I am not prepared to do. I will not use the army against the people. Nor will I allow myself to be replaced by someone who will agree to do it. I hope you can see what I am getting at. Other generals may not have the scruples that I have. They will not hesitate to do what the President demands. If I refuse such an order then I need to be confident that a sufficient number of officers will back me. I need people like you on my side. I am asking you to tread a path that is extremely dangerous. It will require you to join me in disobeying orders from above. If I am correct about your views than I expect that you will know of other officers who feel the same. I am asking you to get in touch with them as soon as you leave here in order to convince them to support me in what I intend. I'm taking a big risk in meeting you like this. I know that any one of you could leave here and report what I have said to a senior officer but I hope that you will realise that what I propose is for the benefit of the country and the population and to safeguard the reputation of the army and that you will get behind me. Be aware that you will be richly rewarded for your cooperation. I will not forget. Now please go and do what you have to. I am in your hands. The country depends on you."

TWENTY-TWO

THAT AFTERNOON the square was a sombre place. There was none of the gaiety and hopefulness of previous days. Many people were still suffering for the effects of the tear gas and there was a general understanding that the third attack, when it came, would be even more brutal than the previous ones. The crowd was smaller too, partly because some people had gone away to receive medical treatment but mainly out of fear of what was to come. The square was only half full but as the hours slipped by the numbers did increase; once again people were responding to the call.

Outside the square things were happening too. A large crowd had gathered in one of the smaller squares about a mile away. They were supporters of Chafik, either out of choice or because the alternative was unemployment; the latter being people who worked in factories in the Special Zone owned by brothers of Basma and who had been bussed in. It was obviously an organised, rather than spontaneous gathering because almost everyone carried placards with the same printed slogans. There was another crowd as well, of opponents of the regime. It was marching towards Independence Square, its number increasing along the way as more and more people responded to the need for solidarity. They had placards too but most of these had hand written messages.

The two groups came face to face at a crossroads quite near the presidential palace. Rather comically they were separated by a lone policeman, mounted on a pedestal, who had been directing traffic. When stones and other objects began to be hurled, he hastily left the scene. The only other police nearby were members of the security forces who marched alongside the pro-Chafik supporters. When that group came to a halt at the crossroads they urged the marchers forward, so that those at the rear began to bunch up against those at the front who were facing the other group. Eventually the pressure proved too much and the pro-Chafik group burst forward. In the melee that ensued many people were injured but gradually the pro-Chafik group was pushed back, as most of those who had been bussed in hung back or even slipped away to avoid the fighting.

Just when it seemed that the pro-Chafik group would be routed a serious development took place. From windows high up on each side of the street snipers opened up with live ammunition. It was not automatic fire and not many people were hit but the effect was dramatic. People in the protest group, as soon as it became clear what was happening, began to scatter as quickly as possible. Some ran into shops that lined the road, others made for side roads. The whole scene became one of total chaos as the pro-Chafik marchers, bewildered and frightened by what was happening, also fled the scene.

That day similar clashes between pro and anti Chafik groups happened in other parts of the country and it was not only in the capital that live ammunition was used. Television screens all round the Middle East, showed bloodied protesters being frantically carried away. Not only did it serve to increase the international condemnation of the new regime but it also made the protesters more determined than ever. Many of those who ran away from the snipers in the capital, made their way as quickly as possible to Independence Square to reinforce the numbers already there.

In the square whatever precautions that could be taken in preparation for the third attack had been made. The shattered barricade had been rebuilt even higher and stronger and the burnt out bulldozer had been incorporated into the other one. Stones were piled up, ready to be thrown and the stock of Molotov Cocktails replenished. Abdul was busy going round all the entrances, wide and narrow, checking that they were all manned and all as secure as possible. Nasir was on the plinth, giving out instructions, relaying news as it came in and leading chants.

Late on in the afternoon the attack had still not happened but then, ominously, the two tanks from earlier reappeared making their way slowly to the barricades. As soon as they came within range they were greeted with a salvo of rocks that simply glanced off. Then, about thirty feet away from each of the barricades the tanks stopped. Those able to see were gripped with trepidation as the barrels started to move upwards. Then, rather amazingly they continued to swivel and then come down again, pointing in the opposite direction, down the streets and away from the square. The meaning was obvious, the tanks were there to protect, not to attack. As the word spread within the square a great cheer went up. People started to hug each other and literally dance with joy. A new chant was taken up, 'The Regime has Fallen, the Regime has Fallen'. Abdul was not so sure. When he got back to the plinth he took up the microphone and urged caution. It might just be a cruel ploy, the tank barrels could be turned back on them again at any time. People should remain on guard. The barricades must continue to be manned. Nothing should be taken for granted.

It was at this point that Aliyah turned up. She had been told about the earlier attacks and the killings and leaving her father to care for Khalil, had come to see if Nasir was still alive. She embraced him openly and tenderly, tears filling her eyes when she found him. It was not at all like the old Aliyah. After they had talked Nasir mounted the plinth to lead another round of chanting and after a few minutes, motioned for her to join him.

For just a second Aliyah stood beside him and then suddenly she reeled round and fell heavily, a deep red stain already darkening the fabric around her stomach.

For a few seconds the whole square went quiet in shock. Nasir, quite frantic with fear and surprise, hurriedly lifted her up and off the plinth. In those moments of silence the sound of rifle fire was clearly heard. Almost everyone hit the ground as quickly as possible but that did little good, several people were shot. Then some hands pointed to an open window in one of the square's high rise buildings from where the sniper could be clearly seen aiming his rifle. The episode was quickly brought to an end. Hundreds of people stormed into the building and found the sniper on the stairs, rifle still in hand, trying to escape. He was brutally beaten and then dragged out of the building. Then someone in the crowd shot him several times at point blank range.

Meanwhile Nasir, grimmacing in anguish, cradled Aliyah and prayed for her not to die. She was very still. All sorts of thoughts went though his mind, that it was all his fault, that her father would be devastated, that Khalil would be heartbroken. As people gathered round a lady came forward, identifying herself as a doctor and did what she could to help. She applied some sort of compress to stem the bleeding and then performed artificial respiration. After some minutes Aliyah coughed, spluttering blood from her mouth. Then she opened her eyes. The doctor continued with the respiration for some minutes and then told Nasir that her breathing steadied but they had to get her to hospital as soon as possible.

Nasir had little recollection of what happened next. Somehow they got her out of the square, into the souk and then out onto a street where the doctor stopped a car and made the driver head for a private hospital on the edge of town. When Nasir protested that the main city hospital was much nearer and he had no money to pay, she told him that the main city hospital was sure to be inundated with casualties from the day's events. Besides she worked at the private hospital where the facilities were better and where she could guarantee priority treatment. He was not to concern himself about the cost. As it was the journey through almost deserted roads took only minutes and because she was able to call ahead and explain the situation, they were ready and waiting for Aliyah. After a rapid triage she was taken to theatre and operated on. It was well over three hours before the same lady doctor came to see Nasir.

"It was a difficult operation. Her condition is still critical. The next few hours will tell. The bullet was easily removed but it caused a lot of damage and there were complications. We were not able to repair everything. She may have some permanent disability. Incontinence is possible. I'm very sorry to have to tell you that she lost the baby."

"Baby?" asked Nasir.

"Didn't you know, hadn't she told you? She was in the very early stages of pregnancy. There was nothing we could do. I'm sorry; the damage is such that there will be no more children."

Nasir stayed at Aliyah's bedside for a further twelve hours, until they told him that her condition had improved slightly and she was no longer on the critical list. During those dark hours he was frantic with fear that she would die and with concern for what it would mean for her standard of life if she lived. As he relived the events in the square in his mind, he was perplexed as to why it should have been her who had been shot. There was no logic in it. Then he remembered that immediately before the shooting he had moved to the side to allow her to join him and it dawned on him that he had been the sniper's target, not Aliyah.

TWENTY-THREE

So it was that Nasir, the author of the blog 'The People Demand the End of the Regime', missed the climax of the events in Independence Square. As the dusk turned to darkness word went round that some sort of announcement would be made that evening. No one knew who would be speaking or when or if the announcement would contain good news or bad. The tension was manifest. Once again the picture from the state broadcaster was projected onto one of the walls on the periphery of the square. It didn't show the same room as before. This time the picture was being beamed from a studio rather than the palace but as before the room was empty, except for a desk and chair, with several microphones mounted in front. Eight o'clock, the usual time for important announcements, came and went. So did the half hour. Finally, just before nine, an off-screen voice announced that the Head of the Armed Forces, General Amir, was about to address the nation. That said, a group of army officers entered the room, followed by General Amir, who seated himself at the table. He was visibly nervous, coughing to clear his throat several times before speaking, beads of sweat on his forehead.

"My fellow citizens, today has been the most difficult day of my life. You are all aware of the dreadful events that have taken place and the terrible toll in lives lost in many parts of the country. In particular I am talking about the attacks on Independence Square, attacks made I must add, by internal security forces and in which the army played no part. I am told that some of these attacks amounted to war crimes and that those responsible could face the International Court of Justice. I cannot tell you how disgusted I am, ashamed even, that the Regime should commit war crimes against its own citizens.

Earlier this evening I received an order from the President to send the army into Independence Square to bring to an end, by whatever means, the protests there. My conscience would not allow me to do this. I have refused to obey the order."

At this, the crowd in the square erupted into wild cheering but this quickly ended as people struggled to hear what was said next.

"In refusing to obey an order from the President I was aware that I would be dismissed as Head of the Armed forces and replaced with someone who would carry out the order. This I could not allow. I will not permit the armed forces to be used against the people to suppress their legitimate demands. In view of this and in consultation with other senior officers I have made the difficult decision to take power on a temporary basis for as long as is necessary. To this end soldiers from my own regiment have seized control of the presidential palace and arrested Chafik al-Baqri, his mother and several members of their entourage. They have been transferred to my regimental headquarters and will stay there under arrest until decisions have been made regarding their future. It may be that they will stand trial for present and past transgressions or perhaps they might be sent into exile. It is too early to tell. Also under arrest are the Minister of the Interior, certain other government officials and certain high ranking officers.

As a precautionary measure I have placed tanks at the main entrances to Independence Square to guard against any attempted counter measures. Military units have also been stationed at key points around the capital and in other centres. All army units are on standby in case of disturbances. I am sure that those in Independence Square and elsewhere who have been demanding the end of the regime will be pleased with my announcements. There will be celebrations tonight but tomorrow we must begin the process of getting back to normal. Protests and strikes must be brought to an end. People should go about their business as usual.

That is all I have to say for now. Further announcements will follow. God willing we will heal the wounds that have divided us and this country will prosper again. Thank you."

'Celebrations tonight' was an understatement. Those gathered in Independence Square roared their approval, hugged one another, threw hats and anything else at hand, into the air. They were soon joined by thousands of others who made for the square as soon as Amir finished speaking. Some brought fireworks and many bonfires were started. Within minutes a rock band had set up on the plinth. Kebab stalls that had been absent the previous night reappeared. The festivities went on almost till dawn. It was the same elsewhere in the capital, in other towns and cities and around the country. It was as if a heavy veil had been lifted and people were suddenly free to express themselves again.

It was Samira who told Nasir about Amir's broadcast. After Aliyah's operation, when she was in a high dependency recovery room and he was waiting by her bedside, he received a call from her. Al Jazeera had broadcast General Amir's speech live to the Middle East and Europe. It also showed the scenes afterwards in Independence Square. She told him how proud she was of him and how she hoped they could be together again soon. When she wondered why he didn't seem more elated with the downfall of the regime he explained where he was and what had happened. Aliyah was not yet out of the woods and her recovery might be a slow one. She would need long term care. Somehow, without saying, they both understood the implications. As the call ended Samira said that she hoped they could still remain friends.

Early the following morning, Aliyah's father arrived at the hospital with the boy. He had wanted to come sooner but it had been too early to wake Khalil and Nasir had phoned every couple of hours instead to keep him updated. Once there he persuaded Nasir that he needed a break and to take Khalil away for a few hours. Nasir took Khalil to a nearby park where there were swings, slides and roundabouts. The boy was obviously aware that something was wrong with his mother and fretted but the swings and the rides soon cheered him up. Nasir however, despite trying to put on a brave face, found it impossible to stop worrying. The knowledge that Aliyah had been pregnant and could not conceive again had come as a complete surprise and an awful shock. He wondered about the child, whether it would have been a brother or sister to Khalil and how Aliyah would react when she was told it had died and that she couldn't have any more children. His mind was also racing, wondering what disabilities Aliyah would have to live with, that is if she managed to pull through. The thought of incontinence was especially horrible to him and he wondered how he would cope if she were so incapacitated that he had to deal with it.

Nasir's thoughts were interrupted by Khalil tugging at his trousers and pointing to the ice man with his rickety cart and pleading. Normally Nasir would have refused, unhappy about the hygiene of the homemade flavourings and offered the prospect of a proper ice cream later. This time however, he didn't have the heart to say no, so they watched as the vendor scraped shavings of ice from the big block on the cart into a small cardboard cup and then covered them with what he said was pomegranate syrup. Khalil loved it. When he had finished Nasir said it was time to leave but Khalil wanted another go on the rides. As Nasir carefully pushed a swing, making sure that his son did not go too high, he was engulfed in a feeling of guilt for all the pain he had caused Aliyah: for forcing her to leave the village and live in an environment she hated, for the terror she must have felt at the raid on their home, for the pain of the punch in the stomach and for the ordeal of arrest. Now she was hovering between life and death and all because he had moved a few inches to the left and the sniper had hit her instead of him, and if she did pull through what sort of life was in prospect for her and what kind of disabilities would she had to endure? Finally there was the knowledge that she would have to be told of the death of their unborn child and that she could never conceive again and that would cause her even more untold pain.

It also occurred to Nasir that in caring for Aliyah in the future he could not expect it to be in the city where she had been so unhappy. He owed it to her to take her back to the village but then what would he do for income and how could Khalil grow up to be the modern thinking person he so wanted? The thought came over him that it would be better if Aliyah didn't pull through, if she died. He could live with Khalil in the city, maybe they might even go to France and he could be with Samira after all. It would solve all the problems. The thought was appealing but Nasir tried to push it away. It was an evil thing to wish for the death of his wife, the mother of his son. It was a sin to even think of such a thing. He had caused the problems and he would have to face up to his responsibilities. His future must lie with Aliyah and Khalil, whatever that meant for his own hopes and ambitions.

A couple of days later the signs for Aliyah were quite encouraging. She was still in the high dependency unit but she had regained consciousness and was talking coherently. She could lift her arms and wriggle her toes, although one foot was much less mobile than the other. The doctors were confident she would continue to improve. The catheter was still in place however, so the possibility of incontinence had not been resolved. That lunchtime Nasir met up with Abdul again in the café they had used during the occupation of the square. News had just come through that Chafik, his mother, Basma and members of their entourage had left the country on a private charter plane. No details of their destination were available, nor whether the departure meant permanent exile or if they would be able to return.

"I suppose it's some sort of victory," said Abdul.

"You think so? I'm not sure. I'd have liked to see them all go on trial here, not get away scot free. I'm not really sure that we've achieved anything much. True, Chafik isn't president but there's no way of knowing how this General Amir will turn out. I fear for the future, that we've just swapped one dictatorship for another. It might even be worse than what went before. Someone said to me not that long ago that this country has no experience of democracy, only of dictatorship, that the transition from dictatorship to democracy in countries like us is never going to happen overnight. There are too many entrenched interests working to prevent it. The same person also made the point about what happened in Egypt after the Arab Spring, the reversion to military dictatorship. It seems that the same thing is happening here as well."

"You're right, of course, I'm sorry to say. We've achieved much but it seems that it isn't enough. The analogy with Egypt is a good one. Who was it that told you that?"

"The person who fed me the information for the blog."

"And that was?"

"I don't suppose there's any harm in you knowing now, it was al Malimi, the Vice President.

"Really, al Malimi? There was speculation that it might be him but I didn't really believe it. How did it all happen?"

Nasir told Abdul about the first meeting, how Saali had revealed the President's cancer and coming death and how he wanted to prevent Chafik from ascending the throne.

"So that he could become president?"

"Yes, I'm sure that that's what he intended but only to make sure that Chafik didn't. I only met him face to face the once. The rest of the information came from ... well, from a go-between. He was quite different to how I imagined, quite charming in fact."

"Even so, you took a hell of a risk, going along with him, given his reputation."

"I suppose I did. Somehow he didn't really give me

much choice. I just found myself agreeing to do what he proposed. His assassination was completely unexpected and quite shocking. You remember at the meeting, in the lecture theatre, how I said that he was our best chance and how we needed to get behind him. Well, we never really got the chance."

"Yes, and how the audience reacted. No one believed then that Saali was our best hope for the future."

"What are your plans now?" asked Nasir.

"I've got a flight booked to Paris for the day after tomorrow. Back to the bosom of the family, for the time being at least. I don't feel like hanging around just to find myself arrested and banged up. Perhaps I can continue the fight from over there and if Amir turns out to be better than we anticipate, then maybe I can come back later. What about you?"

"It's difficult. Aliyah needs me and I don't know now what that is going to mean for the future, for her and for us. Nor do I have any idea what the new political situation will bring, I might find myself on the wanted list again. Right now it seems to me that the best I can do is for of us is to go back into the interior, to the village and try to disappear into obscurity again."

"It will be a big loss to the movement. Why not come to France and we can work together?"

"It isn't really an option, with Aliyah as she is and as she might be in the future and besides, she was like a fish out of water here in the city, so who knows how she would cope in foreign country."

"What will you do there, in the village I mean?"

"There isn't much choice. I suppose I'll have to learn to be a farmer like my dad. It's not a bad plot of land and with a proper irrigation system it could be quite productive. Perhaps I can introduce some new techniques and help to lead the people there out of poverty."

"God willing you will. Time will tell. I have to go now; a lady to see, you know how it is. We've been through a lot together in such a short time, please stay in touch, you're a good friend to have."

Nasir watched as Abdul walked away. He'd probably never see him again and he was quite sad to see him go. It was true what he said, they had been through a lot together in such a short period of time. As he made his way back to the hospital to sit at Aliyah's bedside once more, an awful depression descended on Nasir. The future, both for the country and for himself seemed bleak. Most probably he had simply been part of a process of exchanging one dictatorship for another and now he was going to have to go back to the village and to a lifestyle he had long despised. He thought about Samira and a life together he had dreamed of and how that had become impossible. Instead it was his duty to care for Aliyah regardless of his feelings. Perhaps worst of all was the thought that his hopes for Khalil, his lovely son, might never be realised. Khalil would grow up in the village with all its outdated ways. He would not become the thoroughly modern person that Nasir wanted. No, all in all, it was not the sort of ending he had hoped for.

Other books by Peter Lane

During the 1980s, when the Dominican Republic was largely unheard of, Peter Lane taught there in a school run by one of the largest sugar producers in the world.Dominican Days not only describes Peter's experiences but also sets them in the context of Dominican history. He writes about the island's discovery by Columbus, the relentless geno-cide of the native peoples and shows how the country developed its distinctive ethnic mix in the centuries that followed, Dominican Days is a revealing and personalised account of this beautiful but turbulent Caribbean country.

Vince Viggors, 14 years old, string of convictions, two ASBOs, father in prison, mother on the game. So why does MI5 think he might be their last chance to uncover a conspiracy that could leave millions dead, and what has it got to do with the Holocaust and the Israeli - Palestinian conflict? Vince, was he born bad or did he just grow up that way?

"A super novel for teenagers that uses a fast moving adventure to explore the issues of Holocaust denial and the Palestinian situation... highly recommended." **Teacher Magazine**

And writing as Anthony Merton

Clive, a timid Englishman and the sole survivor of an air crash, finds himself washed up on the beach of another world. There he meets Ggydren, the Keeper of the Door and finds that he must first undertake a quest before standing any chance of getting home again. This quest, to rescue a princess, involves shape shifters, an evil baron, a cowardly king, some violent yobs, an intergalactic policeman, a space pirate and a mysterious community of women who share a shameful secret; not to mention lots of action and excitement along the way. Oh, and there is a metal rod, part of the aeroplane that crashed, that seems to have a crucial part to play in all of this.

Available as ebooks and paperbacks from Amazon.

In case of difficulty email

info@opitus.co.uk